I0653008

CROSSROADS

Ricardo S. Dubois

Cover design: Dixie Press

Editing: Angela Hooper

Back Photo Courtesy: Dwight Moore

CROSSROADS

ISBN: 978-0-6151-5413-8

Chapter 1

Silence permeated the flower-clad hospital room, with only the occasional beep of a heart monitor to break the eerie silence. Flowers of every kind and shape filled the room, each one accompanied with a card, offering their sincere hopes of a speedy recovery. What made this vigil unlike any other that was repeated throughout the world? Who was this man that would receive well wishes from the heads of state throughout the free world?

As you peered over this once vibrant body, now ravaged by time, it would be hard to appreciate who this frail individual was. That he was a hero who dwarfed the likes of Lincoln and Washington. A man who through his personal strength and determination had been a beacon of hope when America had seemed all but lost. The sorrow the nation felt was like nothing that anyone had ever experienced. A nation waited, waited for their former leader to depart.

Pale and in a comatose state, Patrick Hill also waited. Waited to experience the final journey, a journey of the unknown. But as he waited he dreamed, or was it a dream? As Hill lay in his hospital bed, he began to feel a lightness, as though gravity was beginning to subside, arousing him with a sense of freely floating in the air. The blank darkness, which accompanied his coma, was beginning to clear, illuminated by a light in the far distance. Slowly, he began moving toward the light, being guided toward it by some unseen force. As he drew closer to the light swirls of fog, which was shrouded within the light, it began to partially subside, revealing a small clearing.

"Is this really happening?" Hill wondered, or was this journey only through his mind's eye? The light fog had restricted too long a view into what appeared to be a thick forest, in an unknown place. He felt safe, not uneasy in the least as he stood and listened. He could hear no sound, no birds, no rustle of leaves as small animals went about their business. Just silence and the gentle rolling motion of the fog as it maintained its encirclement of the area. There was no wind, he thought, yet the fog rolled. The bottom of the fog was slowly changing places with the top in a slow uninterrupted motion. A sense of peace and comfort overwhelmed him as he began to engulf and savor the sensation. Time no longer existed, he did not know how long he had been in this unknown area, or for what purpose he had been brought here.

CROSSROADS

"Have I died?" he wondered. "Is this purgatory?"

If this was indeed Purgatory, it was nothing like he had imagined it to be. His Catholic upbringing taught of Purgatory as a holding area of souls so to speak. Held in limbo until they could be properly cleansed though prayer, into the kingdom of heaven. He had always envisioned a large room, possibly with other souls waiting like him, or maybe an extended state of unconsciousness until you were finally awakened into heaven. He had read each account of near death experiences, how they traverse a tunnel of light being helped along by loved ones. Joyful for the brief reunion, yet anxious to complete the journey. But Hill found himself alone, left to wonder how long he would be here. His mind began to flash his life before him. The hardships he had endured, the constant struggles and heartbreaks. But through this kaleidoscope of thoughts, he could not help but to affirm his own belief that he had lived a good life. As good a life as he was capable of anyway.

"Then what else could it be?" he wondered, as he began to second-guess his life's journey. "Why was I singled out? I did the best I could," he thought, as his mind still searched for answers.

CROSSROADS

"Could it be," he finally surmised, "that when I was faced with a crossroads in my life, I chose wrong?"

His life rolled around in his mind like a Ferris wheel, unable to decide where to stop first. He searched for answers, but could find none. Only remembering the various crossroads in his life when he had to choose one path over another, now wondering what his life would have been, if he had chosen differently. He realized his life held quite a few different scenarios. Unlike others he had met through the years, he did not believe in predestination, the belief that your entire life had been mapped out for you, and that you were simply going through the motions. Hill believed that we had free will to make our own decisions, and suffer the consequences, or rewards thereof.

But as the fog whirled about him, much like his thoughts, he could not help but wonder if he had been destined for something else. Was there work even greater that he had needed to do. This thought rose to the top of all other thoughts. Was his destiny fulfilled? Just as he settled upon this thought, he felt a strong breeze swirl around him, giving him a sensation of cold.

Then someone appeared, a faint glow at first just barely visible, then he began to take more form, until he was clearly visible. He had a petite form with proportional wings extending on either side. Though he hovered just barely over the ground, his wings hardly moved. His shoulder-length hair lay softly on his white gown, and emitted a gentle glow throughout. Though visible, he appeared more like a hologram that Hill could see straight through. Breathless by the splendor of this apparition, Hill was overcome with emotion and dropped to his knees weeping softly and staring at the ground. The Angel was moved by his outpouring of emotion and began to speak.

"Why do you cry?" he asked, "You are so close to paradise, and there are no tears in the kingdom."

"Have you come for me?" Hill asked, half-knowing the answer.

"Yes, My Father has sent me. But before we go, I must know why you are second-guessing your life?" asked the Angel, his soft voice emanating from a yet unseen face. "You would not be here if you were not worthy."

"It is true, my Angel, that I have tried to live a good life. But throughout my life, I have been confronted with crossroads, and I can't help but wonder what it would have been like if I had taken the other paths," explained Hill.

"Why do you question this now?" said the Angel,

perplexed.

"I don't just question this now, I have questioned it my entire life and have always wondered what would have happened if I had chosen another path," said Hill.

"I see," the Angel said. "Would it please you to see?" he asked. "I can show you the paths not taken, good or bad. It doesn't really matter though, after you go through the gates, all your earthly thoughts and memories remain behind. But now, before we leave, you may see. You may see your life at each crossroad, and how your life would have changed. But I must warn you; you may see yourself in ways you never could have imagined possible. Are you prepared for that?" asked the Angel, wanting to make sure Hill understood his warning.

"Yes," replied Hill without hesitation, possibly not fully realizing the downside of his decision.

"Then let's journey. Journey back in time. Back to your troubled youth, to the first major crossroad of your life."

A bright light flashed and he felt as though he was being pulled, pulled at a speed that seemed far greater than he had ever gone before. There was no sound, he could not feel nor hear the wind, as he was catapulted forward, spinning in complete vertigo then just as quickly as he had begun, he came to a stop just as fast. He was descending now, descending to a place that he immediately recognized, a place of joy and pain. A place he had all but blocked out of his mind.

As he descended further, the old rundown homestead became clearer now. Descending to only about ten feet, he hovered there much like the Angel had done when he first saw him. He was weightless, though he could see his hands and body. He had no feeling, no sensation, just a sense of awareness much like a dream state. He looked around for the Angel, he did not see him, then with a tiny flash of light, the Angel appeared once again, this time only eight inches tall, he sat on Hill's shoulder.

"Recognize this place?" the Angel questioned.

"Yes," Hill responded. "It's the house I grew up in."

"Listen, watch, and remember," the Angel said, as he began to slowly fade away.

As the Angel began to fade away, Hill felt himself being, pulled closer to his old homestead, until finally it was as though he was actually there, and no longer viewing it from afar.

The sun was just starting to set over the trees, bringing to an end another peaceful day. But as angry voices rose, and the sound of objects being thrown and broken shattered the silence, Hill immediately knew the night would be far less peaceful than the day.

The voices were familiar to Hill, having thought he had all but blocked out any memory of those days. In a flash they rushed back to him. Feelings had also been resurrected, he felt a chill on his skin, and his heart began to beat faster as fear surged through him like a bolt of electricity. Beads of sweat began to form on his forehead; he whipped them off with his already clammy hands. A slight tremble completed the entire array of emotions as he remembered. Remembered his childhood.

°"Why did you bring me here!" he called out, just as the Angel reappeared. "I did not want to come this far back. We must leave now!" demanded Hill.

"No!" the Angel rebutted, not reappearing, Hill only heard his voice. "You asked to see the crossroads of your life. This was the first."

"I don't want to do this one!" Hill pleaded, hoping he could persuade the Angel to skip this scene.

"I told you before we started, it may not all be pleasant. Let's watch," the Angel said, just as the screen door slammed against the wall, nearly taking it off its hinges. Hill's attention focused once more on the scene.

As the screen door slammed against the wall, it was quickly followed by three fear-stricken kids running to find a place of safety. None banded together, it was as though no safety could be guaranteed by them staying together, each were on their own.

As the children filled out of the house one after the other, a tear filled Hill's eye. From this perspective, he could see what he had never seen before. The fear in the eyes of the children, and the expression on their faces was one no child should ever have to experience. But experience it they did, and on a regular basis. Hill recognized his youthful self as he dashed from the house, running for the woods that partially surrounded their house. There were neighbors on both sides only a stone's throw away, but this provided little comfort when everyone turned a blind eye. He could see himself now climbing a tree, he remembered how he felt safer up a tree than on the ground, the tree provided a momentary sense of security.

The battle was still raging within the house, as Hill focused his attention back to it. He could hear it; everyone within two blocks could, and as he looked over to his neighbors house, reality would sink in. Their neighbor had been working in her garden, but when the screaming got loud, she simply stopped, went inside, and locked the door. "How I wish I could have done that," Hill thought.

CROSSROADS

Young Hill could feel his heart pounding almost to the point where he thought he could hear it. Was it beating so hard because of the running and climbing, or the fear swelling up inside of him? Maybe a combination of both. He listened as the sounds of the fight made their way to his lookout perch. Mostly in French, only a word or two was understood. From his lookout, high in the tree, the fear-stricken ten-year-old watched, and listened. He could clearly hear his Mama crying, as she pleaded with his father, begging him to stop. He responded with loud slaps that interrupted her pleas.

He cried, wanting deep inside to do something, but knowing he was powerless to stop it. He was the only son, with two sisters who he knew was just as helpless to do anything as he was. They had grown accustomed to treating these occasional altercations like a hurricane, brace yourself and wait for it to blow over. Deep down, young Hill knew this was all they could do. A skinny ten-year-old was no match for a two-hundred-plus-pound man whose judgment was clouded by alcohol. So he watched and remembered how more frequent these fights had become. He remembered how his mother needed her glasses to see and read, and if she failed to hide them quickly enough, they would be pulled off her face and twisted into pieces as she begged him through her tears not to. He remembered having watched, as his father destroyed the few possessions they had, and he watched, as his sisters were degraded with foul names from the man who had fathered them. With his bedroom positioned next to his parents, Hill would have to listen through paper-thin walls as his mother was raped whenever his father came home drunk and in the mood. Yet he could do nothing. Alcohol had a way of transforming his father from a Dr. Jekyll into a Mr. Hyde. When sober, no one could ask for a better father. The good times, however, was so overshadowed by the bad. Though he never beat him, the mental scars he carried would never heal.

The screen door slammed open once more, and Hill could see his father come outside carrying a turkey, with his mother not far behind, still begging him. "Please let me at least feed the children!" But it was no use, he had his mind made up. With one fell swoop, the turkey was tossed into the yard, into the thankful mouths of neighborhood dogs.

"Do you remember this day?" the Angel asked softly, seeing the emotional turmoil in Hill's face.

CROSSROADS

Hill now knew what scenario he was looking at. It was by far one of the lowest points in his life.

"I remember," Hill began, "how my mother had gotten up at three in the morning to start Thanksgiving dinner. She and my sisters worked so hard to prepare the anxiously awaited meal. My father left to go out for a while. My mother knew where he was going and pleaded with him to stay, but all her attempts failed, and he left. I could see the worried look on my mom's face and the heartache she felt. She knew, as did we, this thanksgiving, as with all the other holidays we could remember would end in chaos. My mother kept working, not wanting to show her anxiousness, hoping against hope this Thanksgiving would be different."

Hill paused for a long moment in deep thought before continuing. "Finally, the meal was prepared, the table set, but no Father. We waited, waited to sit down as a family. Eleven o'clock, twelve o'clock, one o'clock, we were all getting pretty hungry by then and my mom could see it. So at two thirty, she decided to feed us. No sooner had she started to slice the turkey did our father drive up, drunk as was the holiday tradition, he started his tyrannical fit. When it was all over, my mother was beaten, all of us kids terrorized, and the neighborhood *dogs* properly fed.

CROSSROADS

"I had come to a point, the point which hopefully few of us ever reach. A point where death seemed more appealing than life. Sure, I had addressed other scenarios in my mind. I fantasized about my mother leaving my dad until he got help. This did not happen though, my mother being from the old school of thought, continued to endure for the family.

"At one point, the devil even entered my thoughts, as I entertained thoughts of killing my own father. No evil could ever make me do that. The only other option was death, ... my own. I needed it to stop, I knew I was powerless to stop it, but one thing could. A day or so later I sat under a bridge. Cars and people passed overhead with no idea what was about to happen right below them. I removed the knife from my pocket and unfolded the blade. It was sharp, very sharp, as I placed it on my wrist. I began to apply pressure - it began to hurt as the knife started to penetrate the skin. Tears filled my eyes as I thought of my mama and sisters. What would happen to them. I tried to justify the act as a catalyst for my father to eventually get help. But no matter how I tried to reason it out, I just couldn't bring myself to do it."

As Hill reflected back to this time in his life, he remembered the feelings and the thoughts that went through him.

"It would have been so easy, but for some reason, I didn't do it," Hill said, as he wiped a tear from his eye.

"Do you wonder what would have happened to the family if you had taken your life?" asked the Angel, as the scene they had been watching froze.

"Yes, my Angel, I've always wondered," Hill responded, not sure what lay ahead.

"Then let us see," said the Angel, continuing to speak as the next scene began to unfold.

"Your mother," the Angel spoke, as pictures of his mother crying over a coffin appeared before them, "would sink into a deep depression, feelings of guilt and despair would soon institutionalize her and eventually take her life." The Angel paused for a moment, allowing what he had just relayed to Hill to sink in. "Your father would increase his drinking binges from weekends to all week long, eventually losing his job and all he had. He ended up penniless and destitute."

As the Angel spoke, images appeared before them, images of events that had not happened ... but could have. The last picture flashing before him was one of Hill's father sleeping in a cardboard box. His sisters came into view in a group shot, as the Angel spoke once more.

"When your mother died, the girls were all later adopted and lived a full and happy life. But they never saw each other again," explained the Angel, as he watched Hill's expression drop.

Hill shook his head in disbelief. "Just because I couldn't take it doesn't mean they should not have done." Hill exclaimed overwhelmed by what he had just seen.

"You see, Mr. Hill," the Angel began to explain. "The sum of parts in your family was stronger than the individual parts separately. Your actions set off a domino effect that touched everyone you knew. As a family, you gained strength from each other, but when the chain was broken, when your link was removed, there was no longer a band of unity. Eventually, your mother left your father and lived a happy and fulfilled life. This would have been quite different had you chosen differently."

CROSSROADS

Chapter 2

Hill turned to the Angel, but the Angel had disappeared. Before Hill had time to look for the Angel, he felt himself being pulled once more. Rushing through the tunnel of light at blinding speed, pushed forward by unseen hands.

As he began to slow down, the next crossroads in his journey began to come into focus. It was high school. Hill could see himself once more, a shabbily dressed pimple-faced kid. His lanky skeleton-like appearance was only partially concealed by his baggy clothes.

"Was I ever so young?" Hill wondered, the cobwebs of time having blurred much of his teenage years. Now, however, he began to remember with a crisper, clearer memory he had not experienced in years. Hill viewed himself, walking through a multitude of students. It was not until he saw himself go into a room with a sign on the door that read: "1968 YEARBOOK PICTURES," did he know exactly when the scene was taking place.

"Do you remember this time in your life?" the Angel spoke once more. Hill turned to see the Angel hovering just over his shoulder. Until the Angel had spoken, Hill was oblivious to his presence.

"Yes, my Angel, I do," said Hill, his voice somber. "It

was another crossroad in my life. In less than eight hours, I will make a decision that may have saved my life."°

"Yes," said the Angel, knowing each and every crossroad in his life as well as he did. "You chose correctly that night, but you've always wondered what would have been the result of a different decision, have you not?" The question was a rhetorical one, but Hill chose to answer all the same.

"Yes, my Angel, I have," said Hill anticipation evident in his voice.

"Then look, Mr. Hill, go back to that day and see what could have been," the Angel said, then he slowly started to fade away, leaving Hill alone to view himself as a High School student in nineteen sixty-nine.

As the various scenes rolled by, slowly moving forward to the time he would make his crucial decision, Hill's memories were brought back fully to those High School days. As he hovered over the scene, he reflected back before this crossroad he soon faced. To the catalyst that brought him to this point.

For many, the happiest times in most kids life is High School. New experiences abound, waiting for a shy reluctant teen to muster the courage to experience them. Also this is a time that bonds are formed with friends you would have throughout the four years of school, and in many cases, throughout your life.

Hill continued to transgress in time, passing image after image of his High School experience until finally coming to a point where he would meet the two individuals that would prove to have such a profound impact on his life. Unlike before, where he had observed from a distance, Hill realized he was within himself, like a second aware consciousness. Viewing each scene through eyes of his youthful clone. Hill could feel every sensation he had experienced in that distant time. His heart beating strong, clear crystal vision, and a youthful body full of energy. Hill went with the scene and he actually became part of it.

"It's funny how friendships for the most part, are joined by social status," I found myself pondering, "I was the pimple-faced, skeleton-shaped boy, viewing a society I so desperately wanted to belong to, but feared I never would."

"It's so obvious," I thought as I walked the schoolyard in my teenage body. "The affluent youths with their fine clothes and new cars would never descend to the level to which I was. Amateur Sigmund Freuds might say the reason I felt the way I did was the result of; "rebel teens of low self-esteem, who finds more comfort in alienating people than forming new friendships.'

"That was a bunch of hog wash!" I thought, feeling myself getting emotional remembering when a social worker first confronted me with the characterization. Able to somehow tap into thoughts I had experienced some sixty years earlier.

"Lord knows I tried not to be pigeonholed into a certain group, I thought, "I tried to mix with the upper crust, only to be held up to ridicule. After a while, I found acceptance with a group who accepted me for who I was, not the pedigree I carried," I relived the thoughts of my youth as I had back then. For the first time feeling every sensation and emotion. I could feel myself trying to justify my situation, as though it wasn't my fault. "So what if everybody thinks I'm a troublemaker and a punk, I could care less."

I began to reflect back further, "Things at home had been one constant rollercoaster. One day, everything was fine, the next day all hell broke loose. I found myself staying away from home as much as I could. Leaving for school early, then not coming home until the wee hours of the morning."

Hill continued to roll these thoughts and emotions in his mind as though he was truly part of the scene, a third party that had somehow become a first party.

"Sure, you may think my parents could have done more. I guess they tried by fussing and threatening me with unenforceable curfews, but it didn't help. I was in a rebellious period in my life, a time when I had to find my own direction."

"Reflect back to your buds," the Angel said, somehow tapping into Hill's thought waves.

"My BUDS," as Hill immersed himself into the past, he tapped into an enormous wealth of emotions and feelings. His buds were just as rebellious as Hill was, probably even more so.

The ringleader of their three-man group was Phil Hicks. Though not a very large individual, what Phil lacked in size, he usually made up for in enthusiasm. If you messed with him, he would enthusiastically beat you to the ground no matter how big or tough you thought you were. Phil had a mindset, that he would not be overpowered by anyone or anything. If you beat him with your fist, he would come at you with a stick, and it would escalate from there until you were either on the ground or he was dead. That's just the way he felt about it. Contrasting this tendency toward violence was Phil's charm. He was a smooth talker, and had the looks that could melt any young heart. Phil was the one with the car, and the three of them would cruise the town, looking for and doing whatever came up.

Ken Bendlow, another running mate, worked constantly lifting weights, and it was reflected in his physique. Short but extremely muscular, Ken used his physical prowess to back up his mean streak: Hill, being one of Ken's buds, had never found himself on the receiving end of Ken's anger, but he had seen him in action more than once.

Hill continued to refer to those days, as the Angel once again spoke to his thoughts. "They were your friends," the Angel said, being able to view his mind's thoughts the same way he had.

"Yes they were," Hill confirmed and began to elaborate further. "Both Ken and I looked up to Phil, he was what we wanted to be; tough, self-confident, and good with the ladies. Girls were attracted to Phil, and he knew just what to say to them to make them melt in his hands. Ken and I, on the other hand, were not so smooth and self-assured. We often met girls who were only interested in meeting Phil, or were friends of the girls who were with Phil. This didn't matter to us, though. Ken and I would try to act tough and cool like Phil. The thin transparent façade was so obvious it only brought giggles from the girls we chose to impress as they left in laughter. So often, Ken and I would stand at a distance while Phil and his newly met acquaintance rocked the shocks on the Chevy. Boy, how I wish I could have been like him. We were lucky to have a friend like him, we often thought."

"But friendship has a price," the Angel interjected, setting the stage for the next series of images. "On this day, you became faced with the most crucial decision of your life. Ken and Phil drove by to pick you up for school, but school was the farthest thing in the mind of your two companions.

The scene began to unfold to Hill, standing in front of his home just as Phil drove up.

"Where we going?" I finally asked, only now realizing we were not headed to school.

"We're going to look for some action," Phil said, handing a revolver back to Hill, motioning him to take it.

"What the hell you going to do with that!" I demanded, as my pulse quickened at the mere sight of the pistol. Reluctant to even touch it.

"We're going to score some bread," explained Phil. "Now, what you need to decide is whether you're with us or not."

I side-stepped the immediate question and asked another, "What are you going to do?" I asked. fearful for the answer I might hear.

"We're going for a score on the edge of town," Ken interrupted, never looking back at me, still toying with his weapon.

"Why?" I inquired further, needing a far greater explanation than what he was giving.

I was caught totally off guard. Just the day before there was not so much as a mention of robbing so much as lunch money. Now overnight, we had turned into the Dillinger gang.

"Why do you think!" Phil responded in an agitated tone, turning to look me right in the eye, before continuing..

"For the money," Phil began to offer his justification for what we were about to do. "I want to take a girl out now and then, I want to by some new clothes. I'm tired of wearing rags and never having any money. You see the Rich brats like I do. Their parents give them everything, and we have nothing." Phil paused for only a moment, as thought he was collecting his thoughts before he continued.

"Just once, I would like to taste a piece of the pie. Just once, I would like to know how it feels to have more than a couple bucks in my pocket!" Phil concluded his explanation, the emotion evident in his voice.

I wondered what had happened to bring us to this point. Was there a catalyst out there that had triggered Phil that I was not aware of? Not knowing for sure, I thought I would probe Phil a little to find out what I could.

"Phil, did something happen to you last night?" I asked, my tone calm, but deadly serious. I knew Phil had a just as screwed up home situation as I did. Any given day or night, anything could have happened.

There was a long silence before Phil finally spoke. "Nothing happened," Phil finally said, his voice cold, emotionless. "We have been friends for a long time," Phil added a short time later, "there are some things you need to mind your own business about."

This totally floored me, there had never been anything us three would not talk about. Now, all of a sudden, Phil had clamed up, and with an arsenal of weapons we were heading to knock off a store. I knew something must have messed up Phil pretty bad emotionally. He was not thinking very clearly. Neither Phil nor Ken were taking time to think about the consequence. Phil was being driven by anger, and Ken was following along as usual. I was rapidly running out of time to talk some sense into them.

"Why are we going to have to shoot somebody?" I said, with each statement hoping to draw them out a little more.

"We're not going to shoot anyone," Phil rebutted. "It won't be loaded. We'll just go in, get the money and get out."

"Go in where?" I asked, even at this point not knowing the exact location of the robbery.

"A liquor store on the edge of the Parish that stays open all hours. We'll drive over there, check it out, if it seems cool then we'll make our move," Phil explained, as though we had done this dozens of times before.

"You with us?" Phil asked.

A part of me wanted to jump up and yell hell yes, let's go for it. Life so far hadn't dealt me such a great hand. My emotions soon became mixed somewhere between fear and excitement. I wanted to go, I didn't want to let my friends down. They were the only friends I had. My mind drifted beyond the excitement of the moment and on to the possible consequences. I thought of my Mama, how she tried so hard to instill in us what was right and what was wrong. This I definitely knew was wrong. How could I every face my Mama again if I did this.

Phil's car pulled over to the curb. He asked once more of me. "You in or out?"

Somewhere deep inside of me at that moment, I found strength and courage I never knew I had. I had always taken the path of least resistance. It had always been easier to follow than to lead. But now for the first time in my life, I took a stand.

"I guess I'm out," I calmly told Phil, "It's not right, you're going to end up in trouble you can never get out of."

"Well," Phil said. "I guess your colors are finally showing. I never would have taken you for a chicken shit."

"Phil, listen to me, man, think this out," I pleaded, but my pleas fell on deaf ears. Ken had stayed pretty quiet through most of the exchanges Phil and I had. It was apparent Ken would follow Phil, no matter what.

"Get out the car!" Phil ordered, his tone vicious, angry.

As I got out of the car I looked at Ken, who had remained silent to this point. I could sense he wanted to get out the car too, but was unable to find his nerve. "Ken," I tried to plead one last time, to talk my friend out of what I felt would be the biggest mistake of his life. "You don't want to do this, Ken."

Ken looked up at me, I could sense his fear. Just as

he seemed to want to reach for the door, Phil slapped him on the shoulder.

"You leave Ken alone, he's not a chicken shit like you, he knows the importance of backing up a friend." With that, Ken eased back into his seat, and fell back under Phil's control "See you around chicken shit," Phil yelled as he pulled away from the curb, flipping his cigarette toward me.

I did not know it at the time, but this was to be the last time I would see one of them alive.

Later that evening, as I returned home, my mother greeted me at the door. Her tear-swollen eyes immediately confirmed my worst suspicions.

"You're safe!" she said, grabbing me with a strong embrace.

"What happened?" I asked, not putting together what had happened earlier with Phil, with the emotion of my mother.

"Phil and Ken tried to hold up a liquor store!" My mother began to explain through her tears.

"Ken is dead, and Phil is in jail," she explained further.

I was stunned, a torrid of emotion raced through me as I tried to cope with all that had taken place. I only got the generally explained events that transpired at the liquor store. It would not be until much later that I would learn the detailed version, in the paper. As I read, it was as though I was there, in my mind's eye, I could see inside the store watching as Phil then Ken entered the store. In my mind, I could imagine the scene and the events that had transpired, and I played it in my head like a film clip.

Phil and Ken entered the store like they had planned. Their pulses quickened, as they became closer and closer to the point of no return. Walking down a couple of aisles, occasionally looking around, trying not to be too obvious to what their intention truly was. Ken patted his empty revolver, making sure it was still in place.

Phil, either by accident or choice, had failed to unload his revolver, no one ever knew for sure. He would always claim that he thought he had.

From the moment the two youths walked into the store, the clerk was alerted to them. It was not necessarily their appearance that alerted the clerk to the youths. It was their mannerisms. They seemed nervous, uneasy, and when they started looking around, the clerk knew something was about to go down.

When you run and own a liquor store, it seems that many people are attracted to it not only for booze. It sometimes seemed that a beacon or neon light, which read "Rob me", is standard equipment with any liquor store. For the most part, liquor stores have the drill down pat. Man enters store with gun. Man demands money. Clerk gives money. Man leaves store. Normally, this is the scenario that is repeated throughout the country every day. But occasionally, there are exceptions. Some storeowners have taken the philosophy, enough is enough and have chosen to fight back. This would be the case for the two unsuspecting teens. Just as they were preparing to rob the establishment, forces were moving into place to defend it.

The heavyset woman in her late thirties displayed no emotion or indication that she had just alerted her boss in the storeroom. She had been through this before. Soon her boss would appear with a shotgun, and the two youths would either run or surrender. Since she had been there, her boss had foiled four robbery attempts and none had ever ended in bloodshed.

Sitting at his desk in the storeroom, trying to finish up paperwork, Jim Seigal saw the small flashing light on the wall. Without hesitation, he reached for his double-barreled shotgun that he kept handy by the desk.

As the clerk rapidly filled the bag with Money, Seigal was positioning himself behind the storeroom curtain. Slowly, he parted the curtain with the barrel of the shotgun, until he could see Ken. He looked further into the store, but saw no one else. He thought

Ken was the only one. Seigal took a bead on Ken, parting the curtain with his barrel.

"Hold it right there!" Seigal demanded, emerging from behind the curtain.

Ken froze for a moment, as though he was following the instructions that were given to him. No one knew what came over Ken, but for some reason he began to slowly turn in the direction of Seigal.

"Don't do it!" Seigal demanded, but Ken kept turning with his pistol. One blast of 12-gauge double 00 buckshot tore through Ken's chest, and due to the close range, the pellets had enough velocity to exit the back. Ken never knew what hit him, one minute he was standing there directing the cashier, the next minute he lay sprawled across the floor, his life's blood forming a pool around his lifeless body.

Phil heard the owner from the beginning and quickly ducked behind a shelf of canned goods. He crawled along the floor until he could see the barrel of the shotgun protruding from the curtain.

Phil waited, scared, sweating at this point, his mind raced for a way out of this predicament. From where he stood now, he could only see the situation escalating. Should he make a run for it? he wondered, but only for a moment. He knew if he ran there was no way Ken could escape, and he was not going to leave Ken. It looked like the only answer was to surrender. They rolled the dice, they lost, Phil thought. Just as Phil began to rise and give himself up and join Ken to wait for the police, the sound of a shotgun being fired ripped through the silence. Phil never heard the storeowner's warnings to Ken, nor did he see Ken turn to the owner with his gun.

All he heard was the blast, which sent Ken across the room. "My god," Phil thought, "he doesn't want to-wait for the police, he wants us dead!" Just then, stepping from behind the curtain into the smoke of the blast, the storeowner now turned his weapon toward Phil. Phil could see his lips moving, but the words he wanted to convey never reached Phil. As the man turned toward him, Phil raised his pistol and fired, the bullet found its mark, sending the storekeeper backward toward a shelf of cigarettes. Phil just remembered the one shot, but it would be revealed later that the storekeeper was shot six times. Phil grabbed what little money the cashier had bagged up, he saw Ken lying on the floor, blood all around him, he knew he was dead. Stepping over his friend's motionless body, Phil raced out of the store.

Tires squealed, and the smell of rubber burning

blanketed the area as Phil made his escape. The escape was short-lived, however, as the police had Phil cornered rather quickly. A description of his car, was supplied by the clerk and a couple of strategically placed roadblocks put Phil right in the hands of the police.

"I remember the trial," Hill spoke softly, "I remember seeing Phil's picture in the newspaper, he appeared so different." Hill paused for a moment, reflecting back to that time. "The self confident tough guy was no longer so tough. He was transformed into a scared kid."

"A kid who stood trial as an adult," the Angel interjected, breaking Hill's reflective state. "He was found guilty then later executed."

"I remember how I never once spoke of the incident to anyone," reflected Hill. "I remember how I somehow separated myself from the entire situation, never once going to see Phil. I removed all thoughts of the event from my memory, like I had never known him," Hill explained.

"But in the back of my mind, I knew, I knew how close I had come. I often wondered what would have happened if I had gone. Would it have been me lying on the floor of the liquor store? Or would I be the one waiting electrocution? These, of course, are the most obvious scenarios, but could there have been a third?

Could my presence somehow have prevented bloodshed?" Hill pondered once again the agonizing thoughts that had haunted him for years.

The Angel spoke, "You need not wonder any longer," he said. "Look now and see what might have been."

Chapter 3

The scene was once rolled back and again opened to the point my two friends and I sat in Phil's car pondering our crime.

Sitting there in the back of the car, I teetered on the proverbial fence. Not really knowing or caring which side I landed on. I started to stand up to Phil, but for some reason I went along, like I always had. "I'm in!" I said, tossing all that I was taught and had learned from my mother into the wind. I knew from this point on there was no turning back.

"Here!" Phil said, as he handed me a pistol. Taking the weapon in my hand, I felt its weight, its coldness, and recognized its potential for destruction. "Is it loaded?" I asked, not even knowing how or what to check for.

"It's loaded," Phil replied, "it's strictly up to you if you want to keep it that way."

"Listen, guys, the only way we're going to do this is if the guns are unloaded. We don't need any accidents." I was firm in my position, for the first time I could remember, I was taking a stand.

"But what if ---?" Phil started to offer a possible scenario where loaded guns might come in handy, but I cut him short.

"No buts!" I said, without hesitation. "I'm not going to shoot anyone for any reason."

Phil looked back at me in partial disbelief. He had never, in as long as we had known each other, known me to be so adamant about anything. "Give me the guns," Phil said, "I'll unload them." Ken and I handed the pistols back and watched as Phil removed the shells from each pistol and let them fall on to the floorboards.

Returning the pistols to his two partners in crime, Phil had overlooked his own pistol, which was still loaded. This would prove to be a pivotal point as the drama later unfolded.

I tried to steady myself, I was scared, really scared. My stomach felt like it had been wound into a big knot.

Phil and Ben seemed unaffected by the whole situation, they showed no emotion or gave any sign of any uneasiness or uncertainty. Looking at them, you would think we were out for a Sunday drive, not about to rob a liquor store.

We soon arrived at our intended target. A convenience/liquor store on the edge of the Parish line. Passing by the business several times, we waited for an optimum time. Traffic was light and few cars had stopped, while we were casing it.

"Next time round, we do it," Phil said, giving everyone a

little advance notice. Phil pulled to the rear of the store and stopped the car. After putting the vehicle in park, he turned in his seat to better face both Ken and myself. "Here's the plan," said Phil, "Hill, you gonna drive, and keep the car running in case we got to leave in a hurry. Ken and I will enter the store. Ken, you take the register and I'll provide your backup. Any questions?" Phil asked, not waiting but a moment before opening his car door to trade places with me.

I put the car in gear and began to ease around the front. Seeing only one car in the parking lot, as I eased the car to a stop in front of the store, we all wrongly assumed there was only the cashier, this would later prove to be our most careless blunder.

Ken and Phil jumped out of the car, running inside. I remained in the car, looking around, ready to sound a warning horn if there was danger.

Watching through his younger eyes, the event unfolded. Hill could feel every sensation, yet he was powerless to make any independent moves on his own. It was like watching a movie, you could not change the action, but what made Hill's situation different was that he could feel the action.

As Phil and Ken entered the building, I could see the clerk had the phone in her hand, as though seeing what was about to go down, but not quick enough to alert anyone. Ken pointed the gun at the cashier, she trembled, she was so scared. "Please don't shoot," she pleaded between her tears.

"Get a bag and fill it. Hurry up!" Ken yelled loud enough so I could hear him outside. I could see the cashier moving as fast as her trembling hands would allow her.

All had proceeded as planned when suddenly I could see Ken's attention shift from the cashier. What followed next was carnage. A loud explosion was heard while simultaneously Ken was hurled backward and through the glass front doors. I thought my heart stopped as I sat frozen, not realizing that Phil had returned fire. It was not until Phil raced from the store and hurled himself into the car that I was brought back to my senses.

"Let's go!" Phil yelled.

"What about Ken?" I questioned, "We just can't leave him!"

"He's dead!" Phil yelled, "And if we don't get out of here soon, we will be too."

With that, I threw the car in reverse and left rubber

for twenty yards. "What happened!" I yelled to Phil, demanding a more thorough explanation of what transpired so quickly.

"There was another one!" Phil explained, "He was in the back, we didn't know he was there."

"He shot Ken down cold?" I inquired further, needing to be brought up to speed with what had happened inside the store.

"Ken lost it!" said Phil, "The guy had the drop on him, instead of freezing like the guy told him, he turned toward him with his gun. That was all it took. The guy blasted him through the window, then turned to me," Phil explained, winded and breathing hard.

"How did you get away?" I asked, not remembering hearing any additional shots.

"I killed the bastard! Alright, I killed him," Phil yelled, tears showing in his eyes.

"But weren't the guns unloaded?" I asked, "I thought you-..."

"Unloaded, them?" Phil cut in. "Well, I apparently forgot one," he explained, in a sarcastic tone. "Good chance I did, or I'd be with Ken."

"What we going to do now?" I asked, panic and fear starting to get a firm hold on me.

"Just drive!" Phil ordered, "Just drive!"

Hill did not have to wait long before his question would be finally answered. As they rounded a bend, a roadblock lay ahead, a dozen deputies with rifles drawn.

Hill was seeing himself in flashes now, each short glimpse showed a small capsule of what transpired after.

"It would have been a tragic turn for you if you had not found the courage to not get in that car," said the Angel, his voice echoing over the flashes of light that began to appear.

Short images of events that had never transpired but could have, choreographing the events that followed. As each image appeared, Hill could still feel the scene as though he was in it.

"You would be found guilty," the Angel's voice echoed once more, "and sent to State Prison."

Hill could see himself in a prison bus just as it entered the Prison gates. As the gates closed behind the bus, an image of his mother appeared.

"Your mother took your incarceration exceptionally hard," said the Angel, as a scene of his mother continued to play.

Watching in anguish, Hill looked at her, not able to

be consoled as she kept repeating the same question, "Where did I go wrong!" she cried, hoping to at least find solace in an answer, but no one could offer her any.

"Your father, on the other hand, was far quicker to write you off," the Angel said, as the image of his father appeared before him. "He didn't even speak to you."

The images continued to roll, Hill felt himself nauseated, and dizzy, not sure if he would be able to cope with all the feelings he was experiencing in such a short period of time.

"While in prison, you made some friends," the Angel said, "one to be exact. His name was Billy," said the Angel as his image appeared. "Billy was in prison for rape, as I recall. He said the girl consented, up until the point her parents caught them on the couch. She yelled rape, and the rest is history."

Images continued to circulate as a prison riot began to unfold. An image appeared of Hill about to be stabbed in the back. At the last possible second, Billy grabbed the guy's wrist and threw him to the ground, saving Hill's life.

"As it would turn out, Billy would become your salvation in prison," explained the Angel. "He would save your life, and you would have a sense of devoted loyalty to him from then on. As fate would have it, you and Billy would have the same release date. This would prove the beginning of the end for you." The Angel paused his narrative for what seemed to be a long time, but the visual images of Billy and Hill continued to roll.

Watching as each image rolled before him, feeling the sensations as if he had somehow experienced each of the pictures he now viewed. It was as though he had an understanding of each scene, as if he had memories of things he had never really experienced. Looking on and somehow remembering how fate had dealt him its usual hand. Then slowly at first, Hill began to be transported into the images as though he had become part of them.

"Billy and I having the same release date, we began making plans to travel the country. I wasn't sure at the time exactly what we would use for money, but it seemed Billy had it all planned out. So once again, I found myself being led, in a direction I was uncertain about."

Billy and I walked out of the Louisiana State Penitentiary as free men, and we wasted no time in fulfilling our dream of traveling the country. Billy was able to talk his elderly grandmother out of her car, a nineteen sixty-four mustang convertible, and we were off. I should have suspected something when he drove up, I just couldn't see his grandmother in this car, but I did not question it. Then when I saw the wire pulled from under the dash, I knew how Billy got the car. But I didn't care. All sense of emotion or right and wrong had gone out the window. I was a hardened man now. Without a home, and without a future. I just didn't care.

Billy and I drove and drove, a different town every night. After a while, stealing cars had become routine and soon I was even boosting a few. We got money the old fashioned way, we stole it. Usually hanging around outside of bar rooms waiting for some unlucky soul to roll. It never netted us a lot of money, just enough to get further down the road. The stakes were about to be raised one night when waiting outside a bar frequented by a Yuppie clientele. Billy would pick our next mark. It was not until much later that I would realize it was not solely for the money.

Exiting the bar was a young couple probably in their late twenties or early thirties. Both good-looking people, he wore a suit, while an evening dress accentuated her shapely figure. By the way they were dressed, they apparently were coming back from some party and decided to stop off for another drink. This would prove to be a tragic mistake. Billy moved quickly, stalking his prey as a wild lioness would stalk a gazelle, he kept his distance at first until he knew where they were going. Then as they reached their car and started to get in, Billy was there at the same time.

Billy pulled the hammer back on the revolver at the same time the man turned to face him. As he looked down the barrel of the pistol, his eyes widened and fear replaced what was once happiness.

The woman, seeing this, let out a scream, although it seemed more like a startled cry than a scream, but she did not have a second chance to yell. I grabbed her around the waist and mouth from behind her, she began to struggle.

"Relax and you won't get hurt!" I ordered, and seeing the helplessness of her situation, she complied.

"Don't hurt us," the man said, in as calm a voice that the situation would allow. "Take the money," he offered, reaching for his wallet and handing it to Billy.

Billy looked at his watch, "I want the Rolex," he said, and once again the man complied, not wanting to give Billy any reason to hurt them. "Give me the keys!" he finally instructed, with which the man quickly complied.

At this point, Billy had taken everything from this man, so he thought. Looking toward me, Billy looked at the woman I held captive.

"She is quite a looker," said Billy, his expression seeming to change. "You're probably about twenty-eight years old?" Billy said to the girl, who just looked away, still trembling.

It was not until that point that I had taken notice of the girl. I had been too busy being a lookout to really observe her up close, but Billy was right, she was a knockout. Tall, slender, well-proportioned features, and the face of an angel. But that wasn't what Billy was focused on as I noticed he hardly looked at her face. He was focused squarely on her large breasts, and did not get much further.

"This your girl?" Billy asked, continuing to undress her with his eyes.

"Let's get out of here, Billy," I interrupted, "someone will be coming soon."

Billy shot me a vicious glance, "You used my name, you moron," said Billy, anger clearly present in his face. "Just hold the bitch and keep your mouth shut, we'll be out of here in a minute."

Billy's demeanor changed from bad to worse from then; on his tone was harsher, his actions more deliberate. I had seen him like this in prison and when he got like this, the best thing you could do for yourself, and those around you, was to do what he said and back off.

"She your girl?" Billy said, repeating his previous question.

"She's my wife!" the man replied with a defiant tone, he saw the way Billy had been looking at her, and knew if this didn't end soon, it would escalate far beyond their worst nightmares. "Please," the man began again, this time in a softer calmer, more disarming tone. "I gave you everything I have, please let us go."

Billy turned toward the girl and taking the man by the arm, he walked toward the front of the car where I was holding the girl, and acting as lookout. Billy pushed the man hard against a brick wall that was just in front of the car. "Stay!" Billy told the man, pointing his gun at him once more to emphasize his point. Billy then turned his attention to the girl.

"How bout you, girly, you give me all you got?" Billy asked, as he softly pushed back her hair.

"Leave her alone!" the man yelled, charging toward Billy.

Billy was too quick for that, he spun around and caught his victim on the side of the head with the pistol, sending him dazed to the ground.

"Put her in the car!" Billy yelled, as he grabbed the

would-be rescuer by the collar, helping him to his feet. Billy reached into the man's pocket and pulled out a set of keys and tossed them over to me. "I'll be back in a minute," said Billy, leading the man into the shadows of an alley not far from where they were.

Following Billy's instructions, I began to fumble with the keys Billy had tossed me. No sooner had I let go of the girl's waist did she try to make a break for it. I had expected it though, and was ready for it. She spun around and began to run, I caught her sudden movement with my peripheral vision and lunged toward her at the same time, catching her by her long hair and throwing her to the ground where she landed hard.

"Don't try that again!" I told her, my tone angry. "The only way out of this for you is to do exactly what we tell you. Do you understand?" She nodded her head in understanding.

I did not want to hurt her, but I sure did not want to face Billy if he came back and she wasn't here. He was already upset at me for using his name, no telling what he would do if I let her go.

Unlocking the door to the Porsche, I pulled back the seat. She began trying to fight me once again, and I reminded her of the very good possibility of her getting hurt. She struggled less, but still resisted, as I forced her into the back seat of the car and followed her in, closing the door behind us.

The silence in the car was strange, the only sound was that of the girl sobbing as quietly as she was able. We both strained our eyes to see down the alley, hoping our worst fears would not be realized, but in the back of our minds, we both knew what was going to happen.

We didn't know if we saw the flash or heard the shot first, it happened so fast. Then from the shadows Billy emerged alone.

His wife went hysterical, trying to climb out the car. I pulled her back and pushed her down on the seat. This was starting to feel like a bad dream to which there was no waking up.

"I have finally done it!" I thought, "I've crossed that line again. I got a break the first time, now this is for keeps. I'm not just a juvenile driver. I'm a full blown accomplice!" Only now did I realize how deep I was in this. Me and Billy would get the electric chair for this if we got caught.

Billy wasted no time jumping behind the wheel, and he began to slowly drive out of town, being careful to observe all speed limits, trying not to attract attention to himself. He drove out toward the country. So focused was he that he never once looked back at me. He concentrated on scanning the area, looking for the perfect spot for the second part of his crime spree.

Spotting a small dirt road, Billy exited the highway, slowing down only enough to negotiate the curves. Dust kicked up as the car maneuvered through the darkness, pierced only by the car's headlights.

After about a mile, the road opened up to a lake, a pretty spot, I thought, momentarily losing focus on what was going on, but this spot, this lovely spot would never be the same again.

Billy jumped out the car, without hesitation. Then threw the back seat back. Only the dome light lighted the inside, but it was plenty. Billy saw very clearly what he wanted, and up until that moment, I had not fully realized myself.

Hill knew Billy had been sent to prison for rape, but like all inmates, he professed his innocence with such conviction that Hill had believed him. He was to be proven wrong once again.

Billy reached for her and she pulled away, choosing to attach herself to me instead, the lesser of two evils. I pushed her away, I could not stop what was about to happen, and besides, Billy had the gun. I wasn't about to piss him off. One more killing wouldn't mean that much to him.

As I pushed her away, Billy reached in and tried to grab her arms, which wildly swung at him. Missing her arms, Billy was only able to grab her by the dress, and with one violent motion, he pulled her out.

As she was being catapulted from the rear seat, her head hit the edge of the door slowing her forward motion and momentarily dazing her. The material proved much weaker than she was as it tore away from her body, exposing her large breasts as she fell to the ground outside the car. Billy quickly picked up his dazed prize, holding her around the waist to help support her. Leaning down, he looked at me with a sadistic glare I had never seen in him before.

"You get seconds," he said with a smile, then led her to an oak tree that bordered the lake.

I got out of the car and closed the door. Only darkness now, with the exception of a few stars shining on the lake. There was no moon, but I was surprised at how well I was able to see after just a short period of time. Billy had dragged the girl to the tree, where he began to fulfill his sadistic pleasure. I could not see them clearly, it was to dark, I could only make out their forms.

By this time, the girl had regained her senses and if not aware of what was to happen before, she was now. She screamed, begged, pleaded as she wrestled with Billy, who was systematically tearing her clothes off, piece by piece as he sat on top of her. I could tell her efforts were futile by the way Billy laughed. Screams, laughter, and the sounds of tearing material now shattered this once-peaceful site. Then after what seemed to be an eternity, only crying could be heard, a whimpering cry with highs and lows. I peered into the darkness once again and could see Billy now lying on top of her. His back arching upward and downward in a steady motion, each downward thrust corresponding to the lows and highs of the girl's whimpering, as though the wind was being knocked out of her each time.

I listened, watched and did nothing. I listened to the sounds of her tears, and a cold sweat broke out over me. This was not the first time I had heard this. I had heard it many times before. My mother would make similar sounds, with numerous pleas. But then, like now, the results were the same. And then like now, I felt powerless to do anything about it.

Billy finished, and calling out from the shadows, he asked. "You want some of this meat?" referring to the girl as something other than a person, just a receptacle of his pleasure.

"No!" I yelled; adding nothing further. I was numb by now, I had been a party to murder and rape, and if I did not go along with it, I knew before the night was over, I too would be a victim.

I watched as Billy picked up his pistol and pointed down toward the girl. It just seemed like a daze, a fog through which I was moving in slow motion with no sensation at all.

The flash of light and the blast from the pistol brought me back to reality. Within two hours, I had been party to a double murder and a rape.

Shaken when I got back in the car, Billy looked over to me, "You ok, man?" As though nothing had happened that he should be upset about.

"Yea, man, I'm ok." But what Billy didn't know was that I was more scared of him than he was of what had happened. I was sure at this point Billy would kill me too. He would not want to leave anyone around long enough that could put him back in prison or worse, the electric chair. So I would wait, wait for a chance to get away without being shot in the back. I didn't know if it was because of his silence or that Billy had noticed a sudden change in me, but he kept making glances toward me, which only served to unnerve me even further.

We were well outside of town now when we passed a patrol car. Immediately, the red lights started flashing as they gave chase. When the lights came on, Billy floored it, cutting the wheel with both hands.

"Grab the gun," Billy yelled, "and throw it out the window."

Without thinking I complied with Billy's order and tossed it from the speeding car. This would later prove to be the third biggest mistake in my life. The first being the robbery in High School that had landed me in prison in the first place. The second being getting mixed up with Billy to begin with. Now, without thinking, I had put my fingerprints on a gun that was used to kill two people.

Billy floored the Porsche once more, calling up all available horsepower, as the patrol car moved closer.

Apparently, the man Billy had murdered had been found, probably the sound of the shot brought out witnesses. It would not be until much later that I would find out this was just what had happened. Another patron of the bar had just walked out and heard the shot and saw us race out of the parking lot. He immediately called the police and gave the type of car and direction.

As we sped down the road, gradually leaving the police car farther and farther behind, I continued to run scenarios of possible events through my mind. If this was the case, I thought, and the police had been able to get a description of the vehicle and direction, would not the next likely action by the police be a road---.

Before I could complete the thought, there in front of us was a two-car roadblock. Billy slammed on the brakes, sliding sideways in the road. Soon, the other police car that had been chasing us also arrived and positioned his vehicle sideways to our rear. We were trapped!

At this point, we both knew it was all over. We were faced with only two choices, surrender or die. I for one had no intention of the latter.

"Shut your engine off, and get out of the car with your hands up!" a voice could be heard over a PA.

I opened the door then turned to Billy, who was staring straight ahead, revving the engine. I was not going to wait for him to come to his senses. I knew he was nuts anyway. Exiting the vehicle with both hands in the air, I complied with the officer's demands.

"On the ground!" the voice on the PA ordered, searchlights focused directly on me.

I spread out on the pavement. As I lay on the warm

blacktop surface, I listened and waited. Billy continued to rev the engine, failing to comply with the repeated requests of the police. Then, all of a sudden and without warning, the tires squealed and smoked catapulting the vehicle forward.

"Where in the hell is he going?" I wondered, as he sped toward the roadblock. Then I realized just as the shots rang out that he was going nowhere and he knew it.

Within seconds after Billy had sped off to the roadblock, I had a knee on my neck and another on my back. My hands were roughly pulled behind my back then cuffed. As I lay on the blacktop, I could hear shots ring out and the sound of a car crashing. When I was finally lifted from the pavement, I could see down the road where Billy had finally come to a stop. Police gathered around the car in a relaxed, celebratory state, some even giving each other high fives. At that point, I knew Billy was dead; if he weren't, the situation would be far tenser.

"In a strange sort of way, I am relieved to be away from Billy," I thought. "But now, I will have to face the consequences alone."

Placed directly into the police car, which had been behind me, I was sped off in the direction we had come.

Fate would deal me one more hand, which I could have never prepared myself for. Billy was still alive! Not only alive, but also cutting himself a pretty good deal with the District Attorney to boot.

By turning on me, Billy was able to negotiate himself right out of the electric chair, and me in it. The story I got from my lawyer was Billy claimed I committed the murders, and that he was more of a hostage than accomplice, though he did plea to the rape, he knew the semen samples would show I was not involved in that.

What key piece of evidence do you think the police had to support his story? That's right the pistol I had thrown from the car. Never realizing it at the time, when Billy handed me the revolver, he had in essence sealed my fate."

The trial was all but a blur the way it progressed relatively smoothly and without a hitch. I could see the jury being brought back in, as I stood on wobbly knees knowing my life hung in the balance.

"We, the jury in the above mentioned charge, find the defendant guilty," read the foreman.

Weeks later I once again stood before the judge, the sentencing phase of the trial. It was here the Judge would deal the final blow.

CROSSROADS

"I sentence you to death in the electric chair," the judge said, "and may god have mercy on your soul."

My already wobbly legs buckled when I heard the verdict, and I was forced to sit down.

Ten years later, I lay in my cell, hands folded behind my head in a carefree manner. My freshly-shaved head felt strange as I occasionally rub my barren scalp, which once held my hair. Death Row was silent; not so much as a snore. Whoever said silence was golden never truly experienced it. It's very eerie. I sit and wait for anything to break the silence, still only my shallow breathing is heard. I swore to myself I would face this day without fear taking over me. Three times before, I had heard a similar silence; a calm before the storm of sorts. Each time, footsteps came down the long corridor. Each cell held a possible candidate for the night's activities, but only one, the unlucky one would be chosen. Each time, it was a priest that let the party, followed by the warden, and six guards to restrain the condemned in case he chose not to go quietly. Each time, it proved they were needed as each condemned man fought trying to grasp hold of life to the last. Fighting to hold on to life, which only now they viewed as being so precious.

"Not me!" I thought. "I won't go out that way. No one

will have to lay a hand on me," as I played the scenario of events through my head. "I will die like a man!" I thought to myself.

Hill's vision was suddenly interrupted as the loud sound of metal slamming against metal could be heard. The silence only magnified the noise, as the sound he had heard so many times before now beckoned for him. "It was the procession! A sudden chill came over him as goosebumps formed on his arms, giving them a tingling sensation.

My heart pounded heavier now as I felt a bead of sweat run from my forehead and across my ear.

"It's not time!" I thought. "It's just not time." Seeming like only a few minutes previously I was meeting with the prison chaplain and consuming my last meal provided by the prison. "Time could not have passed so quickly," I thought, as the footsteps moved closer, each sound brought the party one step closer to me, until finally they had arrived.

The Prison chapel was the first one I saw. I never knew his name, I didn't really care to know, I just called him Chaplain. Behind him was the warden, dressed in his normal black suit, this was to be his twenty-fourth execution. His face was emotionless, showing little expression, just a determination of purpose. Even through his emotionless persona, the lines etched on his face told a much different story. A story of a man who had to witness the death of so many people. He knew about their crimes, but the victims seemed far removed when you looked into the eyes of a man who you are about to kill for doing exactly what you are about to do. But through each execution, the warden made it a point not to let his personal feelings get in the way of his job. He knew his job, and he saw that the orders of the State were carried out without prejudice or bias. Behind him were the others, nameless guards who stood by in case the condemned would not cooperate and they had to enter the cell.

"Back up to the cell, the warden ordered in a calm but firm voice.

I backed up to the edge of the cell, pressed against the cold steel, a leather belt was secured around my waist, and my wrists secured to it. Only after my wrists were bound was the cell door opened."

The guards moved quickly to secure the leg straps, which I would now carry for the last time. The chaplain started praying while the guards finished their work. Then the procession began, the warden went first, then the chaplain, still reading a verse out his bible as he walked.

I was next, flanked on each side by three guards. "This is it," I thought, as my steps became slower, I was quickly brought up to pace when a guard from each side pulled me forward. This would turn out to be the pattern, I would slow down they would speed me up.

I felt queasy, but my emotions were kept in check. "So far so good," I thought. Then a door opened and a brightly lit room was revealed, solid white except for an oak chair in the center. At this point, I could take it no more. "The hell with this going to my death bravely. I wanted to live!" A soft indistinguishable murmur was heard as I started to turn around as though I changed my mind, as though I had a choice.

"No!" I yelled as numerous strong hands were laid on me, I fought, I struggled, I cursed, I tried to do anything that would keep me from going into that room. The end result, however, was that I was physically carried into the room and strapped into the chair. My legs and arms securely bound, I looked around only now realizing the mirror, which was in front of me. I knew there were people on the other side, witnesses to the last moments of my life. I eventually gave in to the inevitable and no longer fought.

A metal shackle-like clamp was attached to my ankle. The metal was cold, but only for a second as my hot body rapidly warmed the grounding device. Next a strap was placed under my chin to hold my mouth shut. It was secured tightly, transforming my steady crying into whimpers. After my eyes were covered, the headpiece was secured to my head, along with the blindfold. This was not for my benefit, my eyes were already bound to keep them from popping out when I was hit with thousands of volts of electricity. The mask was for the audience's benefit. To cover my twisted face as volt after volt passed through it. But as the blindfold dangled before my face, it reeked of a strong odor I had never smelled before. I surmised it was the smell of death, the mask obviously being used on more than one occasion. My body stiffened, I never heard the order to pull the switch. It just happened, then all went black.

CROSSROADS

Chapter 4

Leaving the scene with a sensation of being pulled out of it rather than the scene leaving him. Hill once again found himself with the Angel.

"Please tell me, Angel, am I to understand that one decision, that split-second between maybe and maybe not could have altered my life so?" Hill asked as though, deep down he wanted the Angel to say it was a mistake.

"You have journeyed and seen," said the Angel, his hollow voice reverberating as he answered. "Are you not qualified to answer your own question"

The Angel turned, slowly taking Hill by the hand. Then down the tunnel they went once more. Only now, the Angel was leading him rather than pushing.

As they journeyed, Hill couldn't help but to reflect on what he had just seen. Many, many times in his life, he had wondered what might have been if he had agreed to go with Ken and Phil. Now for the first time, he had the answer.

Before long, they began to slow down, the bands of light began to move much slower now and a scene slowly came into focus. Once again, they were at Hill's old High School.

"But Angel," he asked, somewhat puzzled by their return, "we have crossed this crossroad before," he said. "Why do we return?"

"No, my son, not this one," was the Angel's response. "Think for a moment which other crossroad do you often wonder about."

Hill's mind went blank, he had no idea what the Angel was after. "I don't know?" he finally replied, informing the Angel of his faded memory.

"What single decision did you make as a senior that would change your life forever?" the Angel asked.

Like a bolt of lightning, it came to him. "It was when I decided to join the Service!" Hill responded with obvious glee at his ability to recall an event so long ago.

"That's right," confirmed the Angel. "Now look at your life, had you not pursued your dream."

The scene first unfolded back in High School, I was with my high school sweetheart, Mary. After I left for the service, it wasn't long before she was engaged to some fellow. I heard they had three kids. But that was down a different path a path where I knew where it led. This, however, was different I didn't know how this would end.

CROSSROADS

The scene began to fade out with Hill and Mary kissing on a bench, as the image of them completely faded, another began to appear.

"Please don't go!" Mary pleaded, "I couldn't bear to be without you!" she cried, sending even more pain to an already broken heart.

"I have to go," I explained to Mary, "I want to make something of myself, and the service probably offers the best opportunity for a poor boy like me." I talked and explained, but to no avail, having no way to make Mary understand.

"I do love you, more than I have ever told you," I replied, and for one brief moment, as my heart teetered in the balance, I almost changed my mind about leaving to join the service.

Throughout my life, I would know other girls, and eventually marry another, but Mary had always held a special place in my heart.

There had been numerous occasions in my life that I would reflect back and wonder. Wonder what might have been, if I had given in to follow my heart rather than my head, what kind of life would Mary and I have had.

Slowly, Hill began to feel himself being pulled back out of the scene, until he stood once more with the Angel.

"Do you now wish to see what might have been?" the Angel asked, as though reading Hill's mind.

"You know I do, my Angel, I have wondered for so long," Hill responded to the Angel, his mind still flashing all the memories he had retained of Mary.

"Then prepare yourself!" the Angel cautioned, "You will not like what you see."

Hill's mind raced ahead of the Angel. "What did he mean by that?" he wondered as he slowly began to descend into a past he had long since put behind him. This time would be different though. This would be a journey down the path not chosen.

As I began to slowly fall into the past, blurred images began to become clearer. I could see myself standing with Mary in church. She was dressed in her wedding gown, and the gallery was filled with our friends and family. Slowly, nervously we recited our vows. I was looking down upon the scene, hovering above it as though not a part of it, but still able to feel every emotion and sensation as my younger self did. The ceremony concluded with a kiss. I could actually feel Mary's lips as they gently touched mine, a touch experienced only in faded memories of the past. But now I could feel her, the smell of her perfume permeated my nostrils and rushed sensations and memories back to him like no sensation could. I was so happy, to be able to relive this experience, but why did the Angel caution me so? I still wondered. Marring Mary on this unknown date had resolved an issue that had long haunted me. "Would I have married Mary if I had stayed?"

As the wedding scene fade, another began to appear. Mary and I were in a hotel room, apparently our wedding night. This was far beyond what I could have ever hoped for, I thought, as I felt my arms reach out to Mary. My old heart began to quicken as my younger self kissed her and we began to slowly undress each other. Slowly, I began to descend into my younger self. Seeing and feeling Mary not from above as before, but as though I was really participating in the scene. It was like virtual reality, where you actually feel you are in another place. Only now I had every sensation associated with the experience.

We had dated for quite a while, but her religious convictions would not allow her to let me go any farther than an occasional fondle or rub. But now, in this brief moment in time, a time that never happened, I was able to experience the full uninhibited love and passion of Mary. In the whole course of my life, nothing had ever come close to the passion and love that I would experience that night.

Later that night, the hotel scene began to slowly fade. This was the first time since the Angel and I started our journeys that I wanted to stay in a scene, knowing that I was only reliving what might had been and not what could be or really was. With emotional reluctance, I conceded my inevitable departure and left Mary on that very special night and began to detach myself from the scene and into the next scene.

As the cloudy images of the scene began to appear, the sounds and the smell were the first to reach me before the actual images. I could hear the sound of loud diesel engines being revved up to a point where it actually hurt my ears. Next, the smells reached out to meet me as I continued my descent into the blurred image that could have been my life. The pungent smell of diesel exhaust fumes was the next sensation to reach me. They were strong, very strong, as I felt my eyes water and my head began to become a little less clear, as the fumes made their way to my brain.

As the blurry image began to become clear, the

first image that came into focus was that of myself. Working on a drilling rig, in what might have been the Gulf of Mexico. As I stood precariously on my perch, high in the derrick, I looked out over the water. Nothing but water for as far as I could see. I looked so much older now, wrinkles and graying temples added to my hardened appearance, aged far beyond my years.

As the powerful diesel engines roared to life once more, I could see myself being brought back to the task at hand. The momentary lapse had caused just enough delay to prevent me from laying the stand of drill pipe into the elevator coupling device that wrapped around the pipe and lifted it into place.

Seeing I missed the elevator, the driller, the person in charge of the crew, went ballistic. He could have chosen to regroup and start over, viewing this momentary lapse in attentiveness as a mistake that would not be repeated, or he could do what he ultimately did.

I could feel my stomach tighten up and flip over. The sensation fear often gives you. I started to shake, I knew I was in trouble. Hearing the driller cursing me in a manner you would not do to an animal much less a man, I felt the mixed emotion of a man wanting to climb down and pound the driller into the ground for cursing me in such a manner. The driller knew, like all bullies do, that fear keeps you from doing what you would ordinarily want to do. In this case, the fear of losing the job.

"It was as though I could read my own mind," I thought as I stood on that monkey board looking down to the drill floor. Unlike the previous scene, where it was as though I was actually part of the scene, now I viewed from a distance, though still able to feel what my younger self felt. Now, however, an added twist, I could actually know what I was thinking at the time.

I thought of my family and how much they depended on me. I thought of the hopes and dreams of my two little boys, dreams that could only be realized if I helped to nurture them. The driller knew he had me, and knew I would have to take anything he threw at me. I felt miserable, wrecked not only physically, but also emotionally. Each day was the same thing, having to put up with some sort of abuse. Then after putting up with all that, I had to continue to perform my job in an exemplary manner. But what got me the most was the fact that time and time again, I would be systematical passed over for promotion. This ate at me more than anything else. For I knew that I would be in the same position for the rest of my days on the job. I could quit, I often thought, but quit to where? There is not a large number of companies knocking down the doors of forty-plus-year-old oil field workers. It's a young man's game out here and I knew it.

As I stood perched high above the drill floor, I pondered these thoughts, as the freezing north wind began to freeze my body. Someone once said, when you're offshore, the only thing that separates you from the North Pole is a barred wire fence.

I slowly faded from this scene and began to emerge into another. In the park now, I chased after two boys and a girl. I looked at their smiling faces, how happy they were and how the boys so much resembled me. I embraced each one of the children and felt them in my embrace.

I had to step back for a moment and regain my perspective. I began to view the children as children I never knew. Whereas in reality, because of the choice I made, these were children that never existed. This was by far the hardest scene I had to view, looking upon my own children that would never exist.

The next scene appeared rather suddenly, somehow

introduced out of order, not blending into one another as before. The scene was of the whole family traveling on what probably was a vacation judging from the luggage on top of the station wagon. We were all happy and laughing, but our joy would soon come to a tragic end. From my perspective, I could see what was about to happen, an eighteen-wheeler had crossed the centerline of a hill we were both about to crest. I never saw the truck until it was to late.

I watched as the drama unfolded, up until the actual point of impact, then I had to turn away just as the sound of the impact came to my ears. As I was pulled out of the scene, I looked back from high above, and by the look of the carnage, I knew there would be no survivors. So I thought...

As Hill rejoined the Angel, it was quite obvious he was emotionally drained, still shaken slightly over the scene he had just witnessed.

"Why are you so upset?" the Angel asked, puzzled by my open display of emotion.

"It's something about witnessing your own death, I guess?" Hill responded to the Angel's inquiry.

"But you did not die in that accident!" said the Angel.

"The tragedy killed everyone. Everyone but you. Now look upon the rest!" concluded the Angel, as Hill once more began to view another scene as it appeared before him.

Images began to roll about as though not knowing which one to start on. By some quirk of fate, I survived only to become a bitter recluse, speaking to no one. This would be how I lived my remaining years of my life, shut off from the rest of the world. An angry and bitter man, I drew my last breath at the age of seventy-two the way I had lived since I had lost my family . . . alone.

"That was the path not taken," said the Angel. As though reminding Hill that what he had just seen never really happened.

"How is Mary?" Hill asked, having to know what eventually became of her.

"She's fine," the Angel replied without hesitation. "She has been happily married for many years now, to a loving and devoted husband." The Angel paused only momentarily then continued, "She was blessed with three children, and now enjoys her old age with her five grandchildren. But see for yourself, if you like."

The Angel gestured toward the ground in a wave-like motion and it began to fall away, to be replaced with a mirror-like pool. Slowly, an image appeared, indiscernible at first then slowly becoming clearer. It was Mary! Older, but undeniably Mary. Time had been kind to her, for even through the wrinkles and graying hair, she still possessed the beauty I remembered. She sat surrounded by children and three middle-aged adults, I quickly surmised these were her children and grandchildren. As I looked upon their smiling faces, I could not help but think how close they came to never having existed at all. Slowly, the reflective pool began to break away, vanishing just as quickly as it had appeared.

Chapter 5

"I'm glad she is doing well," Hill said, as though a burden had been lifted from his chest. "I'm glad things worked out for her."

"And how about yourself?" the Angel questioned, "Did things not work out for you?" the Angel paused for a moment as though to let Hill contemplate what he had just said.

"Remember back to an encounter that would change your life forever," the Angel spoke softly. "Look and remember," the Angel said, as the scene changed to a different path of Hill's life, the path chosen.

Slowly, I began to fall topsy-turvy into a past long since lived, only to be relived once more. Slow to appear at first, then gradually becoming clearer. Until I once again found myself reliving this time as an unseen presence, but still having all the five senses life once availed to me.

As my eyes focused, I was clearly able to see Mark. How could I have remembered his name after all these years, I thought, but I did. Mark was an Army recruiter assigned to the High School Recruitment area. His job was pretty straightforward, show High School students the career opportunities the Army had to offer. This he did with a passion and conviction that was contagious.

As he pitched me the benefits of the service, I could feel a sense of reluctance and my stomach knotted up, as I began to contemplate all the options. But as I sat with Mark, I sensed a connection. We would talk openly and honestly, he knew as I did, the options that were available to a poor boy in a small town.

"Sure!" I remember thinking, "I could settle down, get a job, maybe married, but that was not an option I wanted to accept. I wanted to see the world, and do things that I just could not do if I stayed. I desperately want a way out, and the Army seems like the only way out."

I sat patiently once again relieving an experience that had long since passed, and one for which I knew the outcome. "Besides," I remember thinking, "it wasn't like we have a war going on or anything. We are only supplying advisors to a small area in the Far East called Vietnam."

As the events of my life slowly began to unfurl once more, the scenes swirled about like a kaleidoscope being twirled by unseen hands, creating a spiral in which I was being sucked into once more.

As the swirling sensation began to subside, at the

same time the blinding white brightness began to fade into a once-again colorful scene I immediately recognized.

"Do I make myself clear!" the Sergeant yelled, in a tone I had long since forgotten that the human voice could obtain.

Within a moment, I remembered the scene that was unfolding before me once more.

"Yes Sergeant!" the young recruit yelled, trying unsuccessfully to match his Sergeant's vigor.

James Hollingsworth Kirtpatrick the third, (but for the next sixty years I would simply refer to him as Jimmy,) stood there slightly trembling looking like he would burst into tears at any moment.

"Are you a mommy's boy?" the Drill Sergeant yelled, not more than two inches from his face.

"No Sergeant," Jimmy yelled, with the same enthusiasm as before, but the Drill Sergeant remained unimpressed.

In any group, be it social or business, there are always those who stand out as the leaders. Whether it be by mere self-confidence or assertiveness, they are usually relatively easy to pick them out. On the flip side, however, the opposite holds just as true, and in many ways are a lot more obvious.

Shyness, awkwardness, and a general low self-esteem are characteristics that can usually be compensated for, in polite society. But when you're thrown into a group of men whose sole purpose is to learn how to kill in the most effective manner possible, it does not lend itself to quick friendships if you're the most awkward kid in the outfit.

Jimmy seemed so out of place, from the beginning. This articulate, well-educated person seemed to unintentionally give himself an air of superiority, and soon became the outcast of the group.

James Hollingsworth Kirtpatrick the third was a full name that during the entire time we were to be in the service, only I would know. With the only luck Jimmy would seem to have, it had been mercifully shortened to James Kirtpatrick, but from the first time I meet him I had always called him Jimmy.

Unlike Jimmy, I seemed to fall right into place in the service. Its structure seemed to suit me. Jimmy had a more difficult time. He would routinely screw up in drill and always seemed to drag behind as though he had his head somewhere else. Whatever his circumstances were, they were beginning to take their toll on the outfit as everyone quickly tired of extra duty because of Jimmy's screw-ups. For some reason, I don't think I ever really knew, I was far less critical and quick to judge him, I truly believed he would come around. Jimmy had been able to fuse the outfit together as a team, unfortunately they were teaming up on him. It started off small at first, with little pranks to let him know - in case any doubt remained - that he was the outsider. I for the most part was able to stay pretty neutral about the whole thing. I watched as the guys would torment him, and I did nothing. The worst of the bunch was Vincent, he had somehow emerged as the ringleader of the outfit and seemed to take a personal interest in Jimmy.

Vincent Macarelle was a New York City boy from the Bronx, and he always came across as a tough guy. I had heard from some of the guys that he had spent time in reform school, I would never know if that were true or just a ploy to boost his tough guy image. Vincent was not a little man by any means, and I was sure he could probably back up his big mouth with his fist, which I was sure with a mouth as big as his, he had had to do quite often. But still, in the back of my mind, I still wondered how much of Vincent was just talk.

As the days passed by, Vincent became a little more aggressive in his approach to Jimmy. Constantly referring to him as "Girlfriend," and "Sweet thing".

Jimmy just took the verbal abuse and continued to

cope the best he could. The Sergeant knew what Vincent was doing, but he did nothing to stop it and I think by doing nothing, he possibly encouraged it more.

When you shared a bunk bed with someone, on those quiet nights you could almost hear the guy above you breathe, above the snoring that is. Although I seldom heard Jimmy breathe while we were in boot camp, I remember clearly the nights he would cry himself to sleep. The muffled sobs brought back a flashback of myself when I was younger. Scared and unsure, I was either too strong or stubborn to let on. I would be dying on the inside, but I tried hard not to show it on the outside. I think this was the one thing that let me know, there was more to Jimmy than what everyone thought.

Vincent, however, had his mind on other things. One night in the early morning hours, I was partially awake as Jimmy climbed down from his bunk, probably going to the bathroom as he often did. But tonight was different, something was wrong. I lay in bed listening to every sound, and like a mechanic who can detect the slightest ping above the roar of the engine, I, too, was able to detect something above the heavy breathing and the snoring. The sound of footsteps, but they weren't Jimmy's, they were much heavier. I slowly rolled over just as Vincent passed my bunk. He dragged a towel by his side and moved toward the showers in a stealthily fashion. I knew something was up immediately. But what I thought, and what would later be revealed, was not even close to what I would have imagined.

I watched as Vincent entered the bathroom area. Then I too began my stealthy approach toward the bathroom.

As I approached, I could hear muffled sounds of a struggle. I thought Vincent was working Jimmy over a little. But just before I entered the bathroom area, I clearly heard Vincent.

"Quit fighting!" he ordered in a harsh tone, followed almost immediately by, "If you tell anyone about this, so help me God, I'll kill you!"

As I entered the bathroom, I was not prepared for what I saw. Vincent had Jimmy pinned down in the corner of the bathroom, holding him from behind with a towel wrapped around Jimmy's neck so tight that Jimmy was turning blue. What happened next crossed the line farther than I was willing to stand by and watch.

Still not having seen me at this point, Vincent continued with his work. At this point, he had Jimmy pinned in a corner with a towel wrapped around his neck. For all practical purposes, Jimmy was immobilized. Then Vincent shocked me by ripping away Jimmy's shorts then slowly pulling down his.

"That does it!" I thought, springing toward Vincent, crossing the distance in a matter of seconds. I first lead off with burying my shoulder into his rib cage, slamming him against the wall. I could hear the air being expelled from his body as he bounced off the wall and onto the floor. Vincent turned to face me with just as much surprise to see whom it was that hit him, as he was to get hit.

"You're a fucking queer!" I yelled at him, my voice reverberating off the tile walls. No other words would be spoken, Vincent and I went right to it. Vincent sprung to his feet and rushed toward me as though to tackle me. I did not go down though I allowed myself to be pushed to the wall where I slammed into it hard. I wasted no time with a counter attack, clasping both hands together and coming down hard on Vincent's back, sending him to his knees. I quick stepped to the side and followed through with a kick to the face. This sent Vincent sprawling out across the floor.

By this time, the noise and commotion had awoken everyone in the barracks, including the Drill Sergeant, who was parting the crowd just as I looked up.

"What in the hell is going on here!" the Sergeant ordered, as he quickly surveyed the scene. Vincent was on the floor, half-sitting, half-reclining, bleeding about his face. Jimmy was just beginning to regain his senses and trying to cover himself with the tattered remains of his underwear. I was the only one still standing in this conflict, with the Drill Sergeant right in my face.

"What happened here!" the Sergeant demanded, in the harshest voice he was capable of using.

"It was Private Macarelle, Sir!" I started to explain the events that had just transpired. "I entered the bathroom and found Private Macarelle with a towel wrapped around Private Kirtpatrick's neck, then he proceeded to remove Private Kirtpatrick's underwear in what I view was queer behavior, Sir. I pulled Private Macarelle off Private Kirtpatrick and an altercation got underway."

"It's a damn lie!" Vincent countered, and followed up with a badly presented makeshift story. As it would ultimately shakeout after Jimmy's side of what happened was finally heard, the evidence against Vincent was too strong. He was ultimately booted out of the Army, cursing and swearing all the time about how he would get even with Jimmy one day, and with me.

The scene began to be pulled away from Hill just as Vincent was being led out the gate cursing. Hill was pulled back once more to his Angel. They were once again in darkness, the only lights being emitted by the Angel's blurred image, which was obstructed still further by the gentle swirls of clouds that surrounded him.

"Do you recall what that was?" the Angel asked, obviously referring to the scene Hill had just relived. It had been so many years since what happened so long ago had even entered his mind. Now a floodgate of memories rushed toward him, unable to stop or even slow their unabated rush toward him.

"Yes, my Angel. I do recall what that was," Hill responded, in a soft monotone voice. Time once again seemed to stand still as he remembered back to that time once again. Not actually in the scene as before, but more in the forms of memories that rapidly rushed back. He remembered the subsequent friendship that was formed between Jimmy and himself. He would not know it at the time, but it was to be a bond that would last for many years.

It seemed almost immediately after Vincent was shipped out, things began getting better for Jimmy. His self-confidence seemed better and the rest of the guys began to try to work with Jimmy rather than trying to make his life miserable. He and I also became close friends, and he confided in me how an obvious blue blood would end up in the service. It would seem there had been a Kirtpatrick represented in every war and conflict that the United States had been involved with since the American Revolution. With only a sister, and his father running the family business, the responsibility, as he said his father had put it, fell on his shoulders. One thing I gathered about his father, even never having met him, he must be a hard man to say no to.

Jimmy seemed to take it all in stride, he would often talk of his plans when he got out of the service. Since I had none to share with him, I quietly listened. Jimmy laid out a carefully-planned scenario of how each and every event after his release from the service would happen. He would assume a key role in the family business, he would tell me, along with his brother. Jimmy was a planner, but early on I learned he was not very quick to adapt if his carefully thought-out plan went awry, and he rarely had a backup contingency. But putting aside some of Jimmy's obvious shortcomings, he was blessed with a lot of strengths. He was smart, with a good head on his shoulders. Without even realizing it at the time, Jimmy would teach me a lot about self-determination and perseverance.

The rest of our basic training went by quickly and without any major incident. After it was finally over with, I was torn between joy and sadness. Joy to finally be through this phase of the service. Sadness to know that the men you had become so close to and learned to trust would be leaving.

For the most part everyone would be scattered about different platoons, and there was a good chance your paths would not cross again. Or to put a more intense reality check on the situation, ten to fifteen percent would not make it out of Vietnam alive.

As we listened to the Sergeant call out our assignments, I was overjoyed to realized that Jimmy and I was to be assigned to the same Platoon. What luck, I thought,... or was it destiny?

Hill's thoughts left him just as quickly as they had come, and he found himself back to his current state of reality, which was still a question even at this point.

"You were taken back to see what was, the memories you revisited are old, but are the memories of your experience at the time," the Angel explained. "You are about to see what might have been, if you had not stopped Vincent that night," the Angel concluded and pointed to his left.

Hill looked over to the Angel's left just as the dancing swirl of clouds began to part and a small glow at first, and then becoming gradually larger began to appear. Hill once again began to be drawn into a scene, a series of events that had never happened, but could have.

CROSSROADS

Chapter 6

I found myself in the barracks of which I had just departed what seemed just a few minutes earlier. Observing from a distance, I could see my younger self lying in the bunk just as Vincent passed by. But unlike before, I lay motionless. I was able to read my younger thoughts, it was the same thoughts I had earlier. I didn't want to get involved. A short time later, Vincent emerged from the bathroom and returned to his bunk. It would take Jimmy quite a while longer before he would finally emerge from the bathroom, but he finally did.

The next day showed Jimmy still in bed as Drill Sergeant stood screaming at him, but Jimmy did not budge.

The rapid-fire series of images continued, with the next scene being Jimmy in sickbay, standing precariously on the edge of a stool, the sheet already draped over a pipe and secured to his neck. Jimmy had never told a soul of what happened to him that night, but it would seem the humiliation was too much for him to handle, and he ended his pain that night.

The images paused for just a moment to give me a little time to comprehend the impact of what I just saw. My best friend hanging from a sheet. I thought of the children he would never have. The little faces I watched grow up. I thought of his wife who had become as close to me as Jimmy, but now I would never meet her, never know her. The cascading possibilities of what would have changed for me were mind-boggling.

"It's amazing to see how so many are impacted by one, isn't it?" the Angel could be heard in a soft voice, but not seen.

Hill could not help but to agree with the Angel's assessment. Jimmy had touched so many lives and still does to this day.. .he thought so.. rather if he knew what this day was.

"Now see your fate!" cried the Angel in a forceful tone. "See what would have happened to you if you had not come to Jimmy's rescue."

The Angel concluded his preface of what was about to appear and Hill braced himself, for once again everything he knew was about to be altered to what would have been.

The sounds of the next scene were heard before the scene ever came into view. Gunfire, and lots of it surrounded me, not like the sounds I had heard before, this seemed so real. I could even smell the smoke. Slowly, darkness began to give way to light, as I began to descend down toward a large green matting of trees. As I drew closer, a large clearing emerged in this sea of green, and I was lowered to its center.

I stood in the middle of a compound, not knowing this particular one, but my time in the country allowed me to identify an Army compound in Vietnam when I saw one. I looked around and could see men scurrying about. In the distance, I heard someone yell, "Incoming!" An explosion threw dirt several feet in the air followed by several more. Rapid machine gun fire was everywhere. Though the scrimmage only lasted a short time, it seemed an eternity.

I found myself behind an earthwork smoking a cigarette. This was a great surprise to me having been such an opponent of smoking for so many years.

As I watched myself, I suddenly saw my facial expression change, staring in a direction to my left. As I turned to see what could have caused such inward emotion in me, I saw there not more than thirty yards away was VINCENT! My God, I thought, I would end up in the same outfit as Vincent!

As I surveyed the area, I somehow gleaned knowledge I could not have possibly have known just by looking over a camp. Yet the knowledge was there, as though I had been in this encampment for months. In a way, I guess I was. A small band of twenty men now held an encampment, which was designed for a hundred. The compound was cut off from the ground and the charred remains of helicopter hulls served as a grim reminder of how unsuccessful air resupply had been. Yet the group held on. Everyone in the compound prayed for reinforcements, everyone but one.

Vincent had been found out, he got drunk one night and got caught attacking a lookout. The lookout proved to be more than a match for him. Though a great deal smaller than Vincent, he was not going to be his victim. The ensuring struggle that followed brought the attention of all those around. Vincent denied what the young private accused him of, and it seemed a stalemate was immediate.

Then, when it would seem nothing could be resolved, the crowd parted and I could see myself step forward. The secret about Vincent that I had kept for so long inside of me had festered and grown until I finally had to expel this cancerous secret from my mind. I stood before the group and told the story of Vincent and Jimmy, and that I believed Vincent's victim was telling the truth. The group was somewhat stunned, but was willing to believe me. Vincent was immediately arrested and held for court-martial.

The reality of our situation would not prove conducive to incarceration of any of our personnel under a firefight.

So Vincent would be let out of the makeshift stockade whenever a fight broke out.

Deep down, I guess I knew that Vincent would never face the charges. He would sooner die than return home to his wise guys buddies with such a stigma attached to him. So as I lay with my back to the earthworks, the sighting of Vincent posed an immediate danger. He stood on a small mound scanning the area with a hardened look of anger and determination, M-16 in hand by his side.

I guess I sensed what was coming next. I don't know if I had already begun reaching for my rifle, or if it was at the same instance Vincent saw me. Whatever the prelude was, the aftermath took only a few seconds.

The moment Vincent spotted me, he threw his rifle up, which had only a moment earlier dangled by his side. It's funny, I thought as I saw the flash from the muzzle of Vincent's rifle. Bullets tore through my flack jacket and penetrated my chest just as my hand grasped my rifle, I was quickly overcome with pain then suddenly numb and paralyzed. The last image I took with me was of Vincent standing on that small mound being riddled with bullets from all directions. I began to feel weaker, and then I slowly closed my eyes into darkness. A sense of relief filled me, I was free at last, and free from the guilt I carried of Jimmy's death.

A chill came over Hill as it had so many times in the recent past. He knew he was back with the Angel. A sense of serenity filled his presence. He waited patiently for the Angel to reappear. Finally, the silence was broken as the Angel in all his glory appeared before me, shrouded in a warming glow.

"You have seen once more how crucial the decisions we make in our lives can truly be," explained the Angel. "When you first interceded for Jimmy, it displayed character, and character is what you would need later

in your life, when the weight of a nation would rest on your shoulders."

Hill paused for a moment and pondered what the Angel had said. "It is so ironic," he thought, "at the time I interceded for Jimmy, I only thought about how it would hurt me. Not how it would inadvertently chart my path to the future."

"Come now," said the Angel, "your next crossroad awaits you.

"Wow!" I thought things are starting to move pretty fast. I felt myself being hurtled down an enormous vortex, which seemed to spin at a speed that matched my fall. This time I was not alone, the Angel

had my hand. I could not ascertain if he was
the force that hurled me forward, or if it was some
other yet unseen hand that catapulted both of us
downward.

Whatever the curiosity was, it seemed to fade away as
we began to slow our descent. The twirling darkened
vortex, which spun with such ferocity, now began to
lighten, and colors began to appear. Slowly at first then
more rapidly, the vortex gave way to a scene that I
immediately recognized. We were once more back in
Vietnam. But this time, I recognized the unfolding scenes
to be of my memory, for what I was now watching actually
happened sixty years ago.

"Do you recognize this place?" the Angel asked,
rhetorically, already knowing the answer.

"You know I do," I replied, not looking at the Angel,
only the unfolding scene before me. I was standing
right behind a cargo plane just as the plane was
lowering its rear cargo hatch. As it lowered, I once again
saw my younger self. But this time, I stood with Jimmy
by my side. With a flash of light, and before I realized
what happened, I found myself looking out of the same
place I had been looking in. I had been transformed into
my younger self. Like before, I could feel, smell, and sense
thoughts. The only thing I could not do was command my

younger self into an action. What I was experiencing was an actual time in my life, for the second time.

Chapter 7

The heat and humidity was the first thing to hit me as I stepped out of the transport and onto Vietnamese soil for the first time. My shirt was wet with perspiration, but grew wetter with each step I took.

"Come on, Jimmy," I said, looking over my shoulder to see if he was still behind me. "We need to check in with our C. 0. before it gets too late."

"Roger that! I'm right behind you, " Jimmy reassured me.

Jimmy and I hurried through the compound, stopping ever so often to ask for directions. "So this is what we had heard so much about," I thought, as Jimmy and I worked our way around the compound. After a series of dead end leads and misdirection, we were finally standing at the threshold of our new commander.

Our C. 0. was a large brawly man, who at the age of thirty-eight had aged to the visible appearance of someone who looked every bit of fifty-eight. As we approached, he gave us no more than a casual glance, as he pulled a cigar out of his pocket, and cut it in half against a tent post.

Jimmy and I identified ourselves, and having been previously warned about saluting in this country, we stood there not knowing what to do next.

"So you're my FNGs, the commander smirked while he stared off to the distance. FNG, I would later learn, was an acronym for Fucking New Guys.

Stow your gear," the commander said without even looking at us. "You're going out tonight!"

A mix of fear and titillation filled me. I was anxious to get on with what we were sent over here to do, yet apprehensive. This was a whole new environment, and clearly on the other side of the world. It would have been nice if we could have had a little time to adjust, but that was not to be. After quickly stowing our gear in our assigned tents, a lieutenant walked through the flap of the tent.

"You my guys?" the young lieutenant asked, then almost immediately called us by name.

"That's us, Sir!" I spoke first.

°Good, we're pulling out now!" the lieutenant ordered.

We wasted no time in following the lieutenant. What had seemed like only a short walk, the maze of tents, suddenly opened up into a rather large helicopter landing field. Men were already on board and appeared to be waiting for us as the helicopter's props spun noisily. No sooner had we climbed in, the helicopter took off. I looked about the cab of the helicopter. Everyone just stared, either at the floor, straight ahead, or at each other. Every look was a stare.

We landed in a large opening and everyone immediately jumped out into chest high grass. It was thick, so thick that Charlie could have been three feet away from me and I would have never known it. It was night now, with the stars and a partial moon to provide the only illumination for us to navigate by.

Night patrol gave me an uneasy feeling. Our mission was to set up an ambush, in an area, which was frequented by Charlie. We quickly found the location we sought to ambush an unsuspecting Charlie. Clamor mines had been set and we were strategically spaced apart. All facing one direction. All we had to do now was wait....

The cool damp earth initially was a welcome relief, as my weary body lay sprawled across the ground. It had been a long afternoon, flying half way around the world to arrive in Vietnam only to find my first night in this country would be spent in her jungles.

Silence can at times seem to be the sweetest sound on earth, when for so long all you have been surrounded by was noise. The serenity of the forest would prove to be no different. Every insect, every wild animal can be heard each contributing to this wildlife symphony. Not to be overlooked, however, are the night crawlers that make no sound. They do, however, make you very aware by their mere undeterred manner in which they approach; that this jungle is their home and you're the interloper.

A twig snapped, nothing out the ordinary you think, yet it was. My eyes strained to pierce the darkness, but only blackness was returned to my eyes. Just a few yards ahead? ... Maybe? ... I looked over to Jimmy, who had also heard the sound. He stared at me, fear-having Jimmy finally in its grasp, to the point I could see him tremble. To my left, the Lieutenant was sound asleep. Too far for me to reach him to shake him. "If it's nothing," I thought, "no use waking him anyway, and if it's not, he'll wake up soon enough." I lay motionless, my breathing labored, as the adrenaline rushed through my body. I looked at my clamor trigger, it was handy, there were also two others ready if needed. Seconds ticked by like hours, until finally, I saw him! Or was it my eyes playing tricks on me. I had been staring into the darkness so long I wondered if my mind was finally visualizing what it thought I wanted to see. I looked into the area I thought I had seen movement only a short time earlier. For a while, I saw nothing then slowly... something started ... to move! Stealthily through the forest underbrush... It was a man!

I looked over to Jimmy, who was getting very anxious. I raised my hand every so slightly to indicate for him to wait.

Another form appeared out the darkness then another, until finally the dark silhouettes of the entire party was visible.

"Now!" I shouted, as I squeezed the clamors device three times, after the third squeeze, a load deafening explosion reverberated through the jungle, its bright flash lit up the jungle momentarily, temporarily blinding me. I felt for my rifle and pointed it toward the Vietnamese. Smoke filled the air, and my nostrils, as round after round left the barrel of my rifle. Like the last of a string of fireworks exploding rapidly behind each other, so were the bullets. Bang! Another clamor was set off with little reduction in everyone's firing. Soon, the entire area erupted with gunfire. Muzzle flashes surrounded the area lighting an otherwise darkened backdrop. An explosion! I could hear Jimmy scream!

"Help me!" Jimmy screamed from the darkness.
Just as I jumped up to run to Jimmy, I heard the Lieutenant yell the order to retreat. Apparently, we had grossly misjudged the size and strength of the

force we engaged. It was too late for that now. What was important now was getting out of there. As I ran toward Jimmy, I was tripped up by the Lieutenant and fell face first in the dirt.

"We're getting out of here now!" he yelled, pulling me by my shoulder onto my side. His voice was muffled over the roar of gunfire.

"I'm not leaving without Jimmy!" I yelled, throwing his hand off my shoulder.

"Have it your way! We're leaving!" the Lieutenant repeated his retreat command as others in our group began to break of the fight and follow the Lieutenant.

I kept low, rolling over to Jimmy, who was not far from me by now. I could hear the bullets whizzing above my head. Finally, I had rolled next to Jimmy.

"Jimmy, we got to go!" I yelled as the gunfire began to ease. "Soon they'll be coming in!" I said, in an effort to reiterate the obvious.

Then as the firing slowed, someone shot a flare, I'm not sure exactly who, but between the lull in gunfire and the light from the flare, I was able to get a look at Jimmy. His face was pale and wrenched with fear, grasping firmly to the rifle across his chest. Then as my eyes moved downward, I now saw what was left of Jimmy's right leg. Something had taken it completely off. Somehow, the other leg escaped unscathed. I wasted no time, placing a tourniquet on his leg, seconds were precious now as the platoon was in full retreat. Grabbing Jimmy, I pulled him over my shoulder, and I ran. I ran though the thick underbrush with a strength and determination I never knew I had. Running with no direction, and no plan, I knew I couldn't outrun anyone with Jimmy on my back. As I ran, I looked around and saw no one else, it was as though everyone else had vanished, everyone but the Vietnamese, whose voices could be heard getting louder. My legs felt weaker now as though each step intensified the load ten-fold. As fate would have it, or luck, whichever you would prefer to attach to it, just as my strength gave out, so did the trail, without notice I fell off the ten-foot embankment into the river, losing hold of Jimmy as I fell.

The river, not extremely wide and about fifty yards across had a strong current, and Jimmy and I were carried away into the darkness. Franticly, I searched for Jimmy, finding him in the center of the river where the current was the strongest. Swimming toward him, having already lost my rifle and with no backpack, nothing impeded my progress, and within moments I had Jimmy firmly in my grasp.

We drifted in the darkness, huddled together. As we drifted down the river, the voices began to drift farther away. Jimmy was having problems staying afloat, with the loss of blood and being on the edge of shock, I was amazed how he had not passed out.

I knew I needed to get him some flotation support, but what? There were logs or branches in the river, and getting to shore was not the best option at this point. We needed to get as far away from the patrol as we could. As my mind searched for options, I realized I was wearing the solution to the problem. I awkwardly removed my pants, which in the water is no small accomplishment. Tying the ends of the pants legs together forming a harness of sorts. With one rapid looping motion, I pulled the pant leg over my head then quickly back into the water forcing air into the legs as it went. Placing this makeshift life preserver over Jimmy's head, he had little difficulty staying afloat after that.

We drifted for most of the night, shrouded in an eerie silence we both knew would not last. As the early morning began, the darkness that had served as an unwearied protector began to fade. I knew it was time to leave the river. With Jimmy in tow, I swam to the bank, until I could finally touch bottom. Leaning over to pull Jimmy onto my back, I thought I heard a very faint putting sound with an occasional interruption between each putt. I listened again, but there was nothing. My imagination working overtime, I thought, and disregarded the sound. The riverbank was far more gradual than the one that landed us into the river, and I found it relatively easy to climb the embankment to reenter the forest.

No sooner had I reached the bank than I heard it again, the low putting sound that I had disregarded only moments earlier. This time louder, and more distinctive. Laying Jimmy on the ground behind a large growth of palmettos leaves, his unconscious body just flopped to the ground. "He is still alive?" I questioned myself, which stirred me to check his pulse. Good pulse, I made a metal note, then returned my attention to the mysterious sound, which had grown louder by the minute. Lying next to Jimmy, I slowly parted the palmetto leaves, which concealed us. Just coming into view was a VC patrol boat!

The wooden vessel putted along, speed was not necessary during the patrol. But the fifty-caliber machine gun mounted on the bow was. I could see the boat a little clearer now. About three people on board that I could make out, of course, any more would have been crowded for such a boat. As they motored slowly by, they scanned the bank, searching far more intensely than a routine pass would dictate. I knew what they were looking for. It was us!

Just then, Jimmy began coming to, letting out a moan. Quickly covering his mouth so as not to let another sound past my hand, I looked out to the patrol boat once more. "Did they hear him?" I wondered. If they had, we were dead. No weapons and not able to run, it would be all over. I could feel the moisture from Jimmy's face on my hand, as his fever brought more and more to the surface of his skin. Jimmy was struggling now, in what I thought was a state of panic. I clasped ay hand more firmly around his face. I could feel his hands in such a weakened state, trying to pull me away, but I paid little attention. Parting the leaves once more, I looked out toward the patrol boat. As I peered through the palmetto leaves, I froze as I unsuspectingly saw all three of the VC looking in my direction. "They heard!" I thought, as I stared back frozen in what seemed an eternity. After a while of not hearing the sound that had apparently attracted their attention, the boat moved on.

As the boat slowly puttered down the river, my attention was once again focused on Jimmy. Looking down, I saw his hands clasped on mine as he struggled to remove my hand from his mouth. His weakened state proved too much for him, as his efforts were futile. It was only then I realized his color had changed. He was no longer pale but red with a slightly blue tinge. Apparently, during the excitement I had cut off his air supply.

"Jimmy!" I cried, releasing my grasp. I hadn't realized how much force I was using. Or did I? Could I have been subconsciously making a choice? Was I willing to kill Jimmy with my bare hands to prevent being detected? The thought that I could have made that choice now haunted me.

As I held Jimmy in my arms, I searched my thoughts for a solution to the predicament we now found ourselves in.

It had been a ten-minute helicopter ride from base camp, and I knew the general direction of the camp. With helicopter speed of one hundred twenty knots, that would put us approximately twenty-three miles out. Flying out, I remember crossing this river and I believed we were pretty close to the camp. But the wild card in the whole scenario was how far had we drifted downstream. If we overshot the camp, there would be no way of locating it again. I had no compass, no gun, a wounded buddy, and only a vague sense of direction. Other than that, things weren't so bad.

I placed my finger on the side of Jimmy's throat, he

had a strong pulse, hopefully he hadn't lost too much blood. Lifting Jimmy to my shoulder, his weight awoke muscles that had only now just stopped aching. But I had to find some way to disassociate myself from the pain. I couldn't hurt, not now. Heading into the woods with only a general idea of where camp was, I was determined to make it.

As I got a little farther inland away from the river, the canopy of the trees blocked out most of the sunlight, thereby reducing the ground cover. Only a blanket of leaves covered the forest floor, with only an occasional sapling, it was open and bare. I stopped, leaned Jimmy against a tree, then fell back exhausted.

Jimmy was coherent now and in his right mind, the deliriousness having passed. I breathed hard and deep, my chest hurt, not to mention my legs and back, I looked at Jimmy as beads of sweat rolled from my neck and face.

I could see his pain, he did not complain, but I could only imagine the torment he must have felt. Every step joggled his body, sending the searing pain from his leg to his brain.

"You can't keep this up," Jimmy finally spoke. "You can't carry me any farther, and I can't stand to be carried anymore. You got to go on alone. It's the only way, maybe you stand a chance alone."

Quite honestly, throughout all the pain and discomfort, the thought of leaving Jimmy behind never once crossed my mind. He was my best friend, I would rather die with him, than to survive knowing I left him.

"We're going to get out of this together," I said. "We just need to keep our heads."

Having caught my breath significantly enough to sit up, I tried to evaluate the situation objectively, now that the immediate danger had passed, this would be the best time.

"Ok, Jimmy," I began, "we need to do an inventory of what we got." With my help, Jimmy was able to empty the contents of his pockets to the ground. Then I followed, mixing my few processions on the ground with his. One knife, and a couple of melted candy bars were the only thing of use among the photos and papers that spewed on to the ground.

Jimmy picked up two of the photos and stared at them. I watched as his eyes swelled up and a tear ran down his cheek, then he slowly placed one of the photos on the ground where I was able to see. It was a photo of a young girl, too young to be his girlfriend, I reasoned, must be his sister. I caught myself returning to the photo several times, as though to burn an image of her in my head. If we didn't make it, at least I would have an image of a beautiful woman in my head. Jimmy had always been a private person. Even back in basic training, he never spoke much of his family or even a girlfriend, other than there was a long line of Kirtpatricks in American wars. I tried to ask for more details once, but he shrugged it off, "Not much to tell," he would say. But now something had got to him.

The proverbial straw that broke the camel's back. A photo, a memory, had drove him to the breaking point. We all have one, with varying degrees. Jimmy had reached his, as he wailed uncontrollably.

"'Jimmy, "I said, "keep it together, man, I can't have you lose it now." But my words did not reach him, it was as though he had set up an invisible wall between us, where no sound could penetrate.

Whack! Across his face I slapped, knowing it stung by the way my hand burned. That had apparently worked, Jimmy seemed to be more respondent. "Jimmy, you got to keep it together!" I kept repeating my previously unheeded statement.

Jimmy nodded, tossing the photo to the ground. I looked down as it landed. It was a photo of a girl. I picked it up, Jimmy did not protest. A color photo of a real looker. Brown hair and piercing brown eyes, I was not only taken in by her beauty, but her apparent wholesomeness.

"This your girl?" I asked, as Jimmy looked up at me once more.

"Yea, until she sees this!" He used both hands to motion to his severed limb.

"Don't think like that!" I snapped, "If she loves you, it won't matter. Do you hear me!" I said, grabbing his shirt as I did. "You gotta listen to me, Jimmy, you gotta stay focused, focus your mind and energy on one thing and that's getting out of here."

Jimmy looked away, and gave a reluctant nod. While I took my own advice and refocused on the problem at hand.

Snatching up one of the candy bars, I used the knife to cut it in half and handed it to Jimmy. It felt good to eat something, we hadn't eaten anything since yesterday evening.

As the sun rose to noon, the humidity of the jungle became more and more apparent to us. "We got to keep moving," I said. Only realizing I had not figured out how, until after I said it,

Someone once said, necessity is the mother of all invention, and there was never a greater necessity than now. As Jimmy lay wounded, my mind drifted back to High School. My American History classes to be exact. I remembered scanning through a book and saw a litter of poles pulled by horses to carry injured and ill Indians.

Well, I didn't have a horse, but these saplings would provide the poles.

Using Jimmy's knife, I whacked away at the sapling, blow after blow would send small pieces of the tree flying a few yards away.

I had not bothered to tell Jimmy of my plan, and he did not ask. He apparently thought I lost my mind, and he didn't want to deprive me of my turn.

The saplings were soon fashioned into poles, and poles into a litter using vines to secure them..

It wasn't much to look at; two eight-foot poles lying parallel. with six two-foot bars lying perpendicular to the poles, all notched and securely tied with vines. I just hope it would hold together, if not, I was back to square one.

"Well, Jimmy, what do you think?" I asked, with a sense of pride and accomplishment.

"What do I think of what?" Jimmy countered, as

though all my efforts had gone completely unnoticed and unappreciated. "Your litter," I explained.

"My what!" he asked, in a bewildered tone. Apparently, he had not seen the same picture I had. "A litter, Indians used to carry people with them.

"I see," replied Jimmy in a more conciliatory tone. "But didn't they have horses?" Jimmy questioned.

"That's were I come in, now quit yapping and let's get going." I moved the litter as close as I could to Jimmy, then slowly and cautiously rolled him onto it.

I then walked to his head, knelt down with my back to him and lifted the litter. So far so good, I thought, only to realize it did not weigh as much as Jimmy did on my back. I pulled forward, the poles dragged across rather easily, all things considered, this would prove to work out great.

I thought to myself for the first time since this nightmare began, "We might actually stand a chance of making it."

Dragging the stretcher throughout the day, making only periodic rest stops, we were able to cover a tremendous amount of ground.

The sun was beginning to fall behind the trees when I finally conceded defeat.

CROSSROADS

I was hopelessly lost! I had no idea where I was, and with only two options. Either death by starvation, or capture by the Viet Cong. Our chances looked bleak once again.

Facing death, I reflected back to my days in High school. I wondered what it would have been like if I had married Mary and settled down. What would my life be like now? I wondered as I pondered one of the many crossroads I would reflect on in my life. Reflections, and what ifs, the only solace in my final hours.

Then when you think no hope could exist, your prayers are somehow answered. In the distance, helicopters could be heard, a lot of them, it was the base! I knew it because the mechanics did maintenance on the helicopters like clockwork. The same time during the evening, every evening. Part of the inspection was to run the helicopter. I could judge the direction, but the distance was harder to judge. I didn't care though, one mile or fifty, at least I knew where I was going.

Night engulfed us quickly, as I trudged through the forest step-by-step inching my way through the darkened jungle guided only by the sound of distant prop wash, as the helicopter blades sliced through the air.

My back ached, my arms felt numb, but I pressed

forward. Small branches slapped about my face and arms, opening up wounds just large enough for my burning sweat to find. Through this suffering, I never once entertained the thought of quitting, waiting or resting. I was close now, and I would not stop until I was back at the base.

Eventually, the jungle opened up into a large lit clearing: it was base camp! "We made it!" I thought. Having only then realized we weren't safe yet. I reeled in my excitement. I had been told on the first day about snipers in the area keeping a watchful eye on the base camp. "Could they be out there now?" I wondered, faced with two new problems. One avoiding being shot by the VC snipers, and two, not to get shot by my own people.

I hugged the edge of the forest, I knew there was only one way into the camp, the rest was laden with mines. So I encircled the camp, stopping, listening, sensing anything out of the ordinary. It was the last hundred yards that seemed longer than the entire journey.

Finally reaching the road, I wasted no time, this was it everything was to be thrown into this last 150 yards. One of two things would happen; either I would get shot trying, or we would make it.

Like a Chinese rickshaw driver, I ran down the road with Jimmy bouncing behind me. I was getting closer now and could see movement, movement toward the gate. Additional men were taking up position. Halfway, I started to yell! "Don't shoot, I'm American!" Over and over again as loud as my hurt and winded body could. I must have been heard. Because the last thing I remember was collapsing in the arms of a fellow soldier right before I blacked out.

Once more, I was pulled from the scene just as I passed out. It was incredible, I thought, when I was in the scene I felt every pain, every emotion. My faded memory refreshed, it was as real to me now as it was then.

"Angel!" I called, not seeing him at first, then spotting him a short distance away. "Why, Angel, must I relive what I have already done, relive that which is already known?"

The Angel paused for a moment then answered. "As we journey down a road, is it possible to skip any parts? If the path is straight, are there any short cuts? The next step can only be reached by its previous step. So too is the journey, we have no short cuts in this journey. For it is like a straight path, with only crossroads of what might have been. You can choose to stop if you like," the Angel offered. Already knowing what my answer would be.

I hesitated for what seemed a long while. Some

of these visions had become painful to relive. But the unknown was pulling me like a magnet, and farther into its pull I was drawn. "Very well, Angel, let's continue," I finally decided.

"As you wish," the Angel replied, and a swirl of smoke and color filled the area. As the smoke cleared, I found myself back in the same scene I had just left in what seemed only moments earlier. There I was, right before the ambush, then suddenly as before, all hell broke loose. Unlike before, I was more of a third party observer now, observing the scene from a distance.

CROSSROADS

Chapter 8

"Fall back!" the Lieutenant yelled.

Not seeing Jimmy and only having an idea of where he was, I chose to follow the Lieutenant's orders and fall back. As I fell back, I could vaguely hear a voice calling, calling for help! I disregarded it as my mind playing tricks on me. Fear had now consumed me, I could not think clearly. All I could hear was the voice, the voice of Jimmy calling for help.

We egressed far from the original location of the initial confrontation, yet I could still hear Jimmy calling me. As though he had been following us all along. As we were airlifted out, I began to cry. The realization of what I had done, or rather what I had failed to do came rushing home.

"The path not chosen," the Angel spoke as the scene around us had momentarily frozen. "You were wise not to choose this path," offered the Angel. "It is a path of suffering and regret. Look now, as we go forward to see your life, a life that never was."

As the Angel finished, I turned once more to the scene that had once again begun to unfold.

The images began to move faster now, only touching on the most significant events. I could see myself lying in a bunk aboard ship. Saigon had fallen, the war was over. I was going home . But home to what? As I lay in the bunk staring at the wall, all I could think of was the thousands of men we were leaving behind. MIA, the military official classification for Missing in Action. Did Jimmy survive and was he being held in a prison somewhere? I never should have left him, I tormented myself. The war had taken a heavy toll on me, though physically I was able to come through unscathed. Emotionally, I was a wreak.

The next scene showed a variety of short flashes of the many jobs in which I could not manage to hold onto. Bouncing from job to job, mostly manual labor until age finally put a stop to even that.

I could see myself on the street now destitute, surviving on scraps from trash bins. I eventually landed in our Nation's Capital full of rich Washington-types who ultimately landed me in the situation I was in. I was bitter now, angry with everyone and everything, and blamed everyone for my trouble but myself. I often found myself in jail, unable to control the hostility that had grown inside of me for so many years.

I was approaching forty-five, as the Washington winter began to close in on me. I had become extremely paranoid at this point, thinking people were watching me and following me. I never would know if my paranoia was founded or not. For as I laid on that park bench, a ragged dirty veteran from a war everyone wanted to forget, I began to feel a sense of peace, as the rapidly dropping temperature began to penetrate the few garments that wrapped my body. I spent my last night on earth across from the White House, retracing my life in my mind. "What would my life have been like," I wondered, "if I had made different choices?" I wondered, but found no answer as hypothermia closed in and I drifted off to sleep. I would be found the next morning frozen to death. I would leave nothing behind and by the next day, it would have been as though I had never existed at all.

I shuddered as the scene began to fade away. That's terrible I thought, to myself.

"It is terrible," the Angel agreed, being able to read my thoughts.

"A path not chosen, a life not lived," the Angel once again explained all that had happened.

"By not saving Jimmy, you embarked on a path that led only to pain and self-doubt. It is not only Jimmy that ultimately will hold the key to your success. It is the confidence and determination you find within yourself. After going through what you ultimately would go through with Jimmy, you know that anything can be achieved through gut strength and perseverance. It was a pivotal point in your life, and one that you had chosen correctly," The Angel concluded, looking away as though to prepare for the next crossroad.

I watched intently, wondering what the next crossroad would be like. Would it be a little more positive than what I had experienced thus far? I would not have to wonder long, the Angel motioned me forward.

"Relive once again what was your life, as you stood on a crossroad of fate," the Angel offered, then motioned to a light that began to appear, and the images within started to become clear. I fell into yet another crossroad; my only solace was this was a flashback of the life I lived, the path I chose. I knew, however, the path not taken lay ahead, and I shuddered at what that may be.

No sooner had the words left my mouth, then I felt the pull of the Angel's hand. A pull I was growing accustomed to as the tunnel of lights moved faster and faster. Finally, after a period of time I could not judge, the forward motion began to slow, and the images of my past came into focus.

Chapter 9

It was Jimmy, he and I was having coffee. I remembered the day, it truly was a turning point in my life. I looked on as the scene once again appeared before me. I was in New Orleans, at a small cafe called Cafe du Mon. I looked on, as the scene began to take on a life of its own, and like before, I went along for the ride.

"How does it feel to be a civilian again?" Jimmy asked, as I sipped on my coffee.

"Too early to tell," I responded, knowing Jimmy knew I was glad to be out. "The service had been somewhat of a disappointment for me."

"Disappointed!" Jimmy exclaimed in surprise. "You were the most gung ho man I ever met, you won a Purple Heart and a Congressional Medal of Honor for our trek trough the jungle. Which by the way I never thanked you for saving my life.

"I don't know, Jimmy, I thought the service would open up some opportunities for me. I don't want to go back home, it would be like making a complete circle right back where I started." I tried to explain to Jimmy the dilemma I now found myself in and he listened with empathy, but knowing Jimmy the way I did, I suspected something else was going on. Jimmy didn't meet with me to talk about old times, he had an agenda. I waited for him to spring it, I didn't have to wait long.

"You may not have to," Jimmy offered, his tone serious now as he leaned back in his chair. "I owe you a debt I can never repay, but beyond that, you're my friend. Remember during boot camp how the guys used to harass me about having a silver spoon up my ass. Well, they weren't wrong, so to speak. I spoke about my family only in the most general terms. You know my father owns a boat business?"

"Yea, you told me that, charter cruise, stuff like that?" I replied, reflecting back to the vague explanation Jimmy had given of the family business.

"Not exactly," said Jimmy, and began to explain. "We own a shipyard, a big one. I never planned to be in the service, I never wanted it, but when my number came up, I had to. My father would have disowned me if I had disgraced him by running to Canada. He was a fighter pilot during World War Two, and his father was in World War One. He believes very strongly in service to country."

I tried to remember some of the conversations Jimmy and I had about his family, and did remember the part of his father. I guess it stuck out in my mind.

"Well, let's cut to the chase," Jimmy said obviously

getting a little more exited at this point. "I talked to my dad about you, and he wants me to bring you into the company."

I paused for a moment trying to think what skill I would have to bring to Jimmy's family business. I had none, and Jimmy knew this. I was now even more puzzled by his offer. Maybe it was some type of trainee position? They would teach me how to weld? My dad had been a welder in shipyards as long as I could remember. I had always sworn I would never have a life like that.

"Jimmy, I can't tell you how much I appreciate the offer, but my dad was a welder in a shipyard, I swore I would not go down the same path he did." My tone was as appreciative and as conciliatory as I could possible come across. Jimmy would understand and that would be the end of it I thought. But I was not prepared for what Jimmy was to counter with.

"I understand," Jimmy sighed, as though disappointed. Then in what was to be his typical operating style, he blind-sided me when I least expected it. "I didn't know your dad was a junior executive for a ship yard," Jimmy sprung the snare.

"What!" I exclaimed, "a junior what?"

"A junior executive," Jimmy expanded.

"A junior executive? But, Jimmy, I don't know anything about ship building."

"You don't have to, you'll learn as you go. Besides, the offer is coming directly from my father."

I thought for a moment and realized how good an offer Jimmy was making me. My immediate instinct was to say yes. But just when I was about to shake Jimmy's hand on it, pride reared its ugly head. "I don't know, Jimmy, I sense your father might be doing this out of some obligation you or he feels toward me."

"Believe me when I tell you," Jimmy explained, "You're my best friend in the world, and I only offered your name to my father out of friendship, but the final decision was his. And believe me, he does nothing out of obligation. He has an ulterior motive that even I have not been able to discover."

Jimmy was being very up front with me, he had told me what a strong businessman his father was. But what could he possibly want with me? I wondered. "Look, don't answer now, sleep on it. Give me your answer later. Where are your bags?" Jimmy asked, looking around.

"They're at the hotel," I informed him, seeing him visually surprised.

"Hotel!" Jimmy exclaimed, "I assumed you would stay with me."

"You never said," I started to explain, "I did not assume."

"Well, we'll assume our way over there and get your bags," Jimmy said, taking charge in a manner I had not seen in him before.

"But ---" was the only word I could get out before being cut off by Jimmy.

"I'll hear nothing of it," he said, rising from his chair. "My family is expecting you." I looked at Jimmy's leg as he rose, you could not even tell he had a prosthesis at all.

After retrieving my bags, Jimmy and I left New Orleans and headed west out of town. It was the first time I had ever ridden in a Mercedes, and to be quite honest, I sort of liked it.

"This yours?" I asked Jimmy as he weaved in and out of traffic. "Yes," he replied rather nonchalantly. "But it's not my favorite."

As tight-lipped and secretive Jimmy had kept his wealth in basic training, he had no problem flaunting it now. Leaving the city, we turned onto Causeway Boulevard, which led to the Ponchatrain Causeway, the world's longest bridge. Over twenty-five miles, straight as an arrow. As I would later find out, Jimmy lived with his family on the other side of this great mass of water, in a town known as Mandeville. In recent years, Mandeville had become the place for the wealthy to live. It proved far enough from the city to escape the crime and urban blight, yet close enough to commute, for those who maintained a business in the city. As we drove across the Lake, we talked mostly of our basic training days, the trouble we got into, and the pranks we pulled. Jimmy said nothing about Vietnam, nor did I.

I looked hard at Jimmy as we drove across the great body of water. His tailored-made suit, manicured hands, and neatly trimmed hair each sent the message of a well-maintained man of privilege. Everyone always summed him up as a rich kid, I guess even I did, though I didn't want to admit it. I guess in part, I knew I would never have been a friend with him if I had. Too much resentment still lingered inside of me toward the rich. People so often looked down upon me when I was younger. It was a time of deep resentment and hatred, some of which I apparently still carried with me. But Jimmy was alright with me. We had been through hell together and had bonded a friendship, which would be difficult to sever, even by my resentment and paranoia.

When we first turned into the drive, I thought it was just another road. We had turned down several, passing large estates set far from the road, with high iron fences marking their borders. But there were no fences around Jimmy's house. We drove down the drive that was nestled within oaks lining each side of the drive, forming a canopy overhead. Only on occasional void emitted direct sunlight, the rest was diffused. As we rounded a bend, Jimmy's house began to appear. From this point on, we'll have to refer to Jimmy's humble dwelling by a more adequate description, "Mansion."

It was a tremendous Victorian home two stories tall, the center of the roof formed a fish scale gable that faced forward. Flanked on each side by towers, which extended all the way to the first floor, rounding its corners. Wrapped by a ten-foot porch, which was about three feet off the ground, the house was picturesque, among the two hundred-year-old living oaks. The yard appeared to be meticulously landscaped with flowers and scrubs, and obviously maintained at great cost.

I was totally taken back; there's rich, then there's the super rich. Apparently, I had underestimated my friend. We parked right in front of the house and casually strolled up the front porch. Upon entering through the front door, one immediately noticed the fine furnishing, all of which was restored antiques, I had never in my entire life ever set foot in a mansion such as this.

I followed Jimmy into the parlor, there to greet us was

his family standing in a row as though to greet some dignitary. All were immaculately dressed. I immediately felt out of place. Jimmy's father was much older than I had expected, probably in his late seventies, white haired with a large handlebar mustache, he flashed a broad smile upon seeing me. His mother was a good deal younger than his father, probably round forty-two and times had been good to her. She still projected a beauty and air about her, which I was sure, could still turn many a head. The third lady, I recognized from a photo seen only once on a jungle floor in Vietnam, yet somehow it had burned its image in my mind. She was beautiful, a photograph could give no justice to her person, yet something was not right. Looking into her eyes in an unintentional stare, I could see her deep brown eyes had a glaze on them. I was oh too familiar with the cause, I had seen it many times in my drunken father's eyes.

Breaking our stare, I turned my attention to Jimmy's father, who had extended his hand.

The stare had broken my concentration and I missed Jimmy's formal introduction.

"Sir, I can't tell you what an honor it is to meet the man that saved my son's life." Mr. Kirtpatrick stated, shaking my hand. His grip was firm and strong, not like some bankers I've shaken hands with. My experience had been; shaking hands with people with money was like shaking hands with a wet dishtowel.

"Pleased to meet you, Sir," I politely replied, as Jimmy prepared to introduce a woman I assumed to be his mother.

"May I introduce my mother," said Jimmy, obviously well rehearsed in introductions.

"Mam," I said, while simultaneously nodding my head, as she extended her hand. I didn't know whether to kiss it or to shake it. I ended up doing neither, placing her hand in mine. I slowly placed the other on top as I nodded.

As we moved to the last remaining lady in line, I broke off Jimmy's introduction.

"And this must be Maggie," I offered in speculation. She did not extend her hand nor did I offer mine, we simple nodded.

"You speak my name as though you know me," She snapped her response in an abrasive tone, obviously surprised that I knew her name.

"Excuse me, Mam," I quickly replied in an effort to calm her. "I remember Jimmy used to talk about you,- and I saw your picture once. You must forgive my poor manners," I said, apologizing sincerely. I did not want to embarrass my friend in front of his family, yet I felt I had.

I was not used to all this formality, it weighed on me like a lead overcoat.

"It's ok!" Jimmy cut in, "Maggie is just displaying one of her less admirable attributes, her obnoxiousness."

Maggie turned red, and immediately stormed out the room without saying another word. Jimmy turned to his mother.

"I'm sorry, dear," Jimmy's mother whispered, "I tried to get her not to drink so much, but she would...."

Mrs. Kirtpatrick's words were soft but due to my close proximity, they were easily heard. His father looked on without saying a word. After a few awkward moments, Mr. Kirtpatrick walked over to me. Without saying a word, he took me by the shoulder and led me out the room.

I couldn't believe it! I thought, I was in his home for only five minutes and found myself right in the middle of a family quarrel, though mild compared to what I was accustomed to.

"You know I was in the service," Mr. Kirtpatrick began as we walked into what appeared to be his study, though I was not sure what name they had attached to this room. "World War Two, I was a fighter pilot, shot down twice." As we fully entered the room, the decor began to take on an overwhelming since of history, and service to country. Photos and war memorabilia dating back to the Civil War lined the paneled walls. Each photo had a name, a story, and a connection to the family. Each bayonet, and sword had its own individual story, which Mr. Kirtpatrick projected energy and enthusiasm I had only seen in professional tour guides.

We would be in the room for quite a while, losing track of time. I had been totally taken in by Mr. Kirtpatrick's stories and a part of me wanted him to continue until each and every story could be heard.

Jimmy returned in what he thought was to be a rescue attempt. Little did he really know how interesting I found the stories.

"Father," Jimmy interrupted, "I'll show our guest his room, we can all get acquainted later."

"Very well then," Mr. Kirtpatrick said, as he turned toward me, once again extending his hand, "Later, son."

I followed Jimmy up the steps to the room he had prepared for me. A suite would have more adequately described it. It was very spacious with a queen-sized bed and two chairs by the bay window, with a private bath. I immediately noticed the suit on the bed, but waited for Jimmy to explain.

"Listen," Jimmy began, "I'm sorry about my wife, she drinks a ..."

"No apology necessary," I said, cutting him off before he could finish, "My manners were bad."

"No they weren't!" Jimmy rebutted, "But thanks for understanding." Turning to the suit lying on the bed, Jimmy motioned toward it. "We normally dress for dinner, but if it makes you uncomfortable, you can come casual

"No," I quickly replied, "when in Rome, do like the Romans do," the cliché popped into my head.

"Well then, I laid a suit out for you. It should fit, we're still about the same size."

"Thank you, Jimmy, " I once again expressed my appreciation.

"It's good to see you again," Jimmy said, putting his hand on my shoulder then leaving the room.

Dinner was quite cordial considering the rough beginning everyone had earlier. Half way through dinner, a cheerful greeting interrupted us.

"Sorry I'm late, everyone," the pleasant voice announced as I turned to see the source of our interruption. There standing not more than three feet away was another image I had carried with me for so many years. I had seen her also only once in a photograph, the same time I had seen Maggie's. Though older than what I remembered in the photo, still unmistakably Jimmy's younger sister, and more gorgeous than I could have possibly imagined.

The men rose as she entered, and Jimmy introduced her as his baby sister, Emily. "Pleased to meet you," she replied, extending her hand to shake mine.

"The pleasure is surely mine," I countered, as our eyes meet and locked on one another. We must have stared at each other for some time, I could not recall when we had began. The sound of Jimmy clearing his throat brought me back to reality. I pulled Emily's chair out for her as she sat next to me.

I tried not to be to obvious, but all through dinner I used every opportunity to sneak a peek at Emily, and engage her in conversation as much as possible. I had never been taken back by someone as much as I had her.

Upon the conclusion of the meal, Jimmy, Mr. Kirtpatrick, and myself retreated to what they referred to as the parlor for an after dinner drink and cigar.

Offering a cigar to each of us, Mr. Kirtpatrick returned the box to the shelf. Slowly, he passed the cigar in front of his nose and paused momentarily as though in deep thought. Then as though he had finally corralled all his thoughts, he finally said, "Nobody makes a cigar like a Cuban." Not being a cigar aficionado, I had no idea what he was talking about.

"I've heard a great deal about you from Jimmy," Mr. Kirtpatrick began, swirls of smoke from the freshly lit cigar started upward.

I said nothing at this point, reasoning I could learn far more if I listened, than if I muddied the water by talking.

"I truly hope you'll consider our offer. We could use someone like you," Mr. Kirtpatrick explained, not realizing he just set off a bomb inside of me. Ignited by the buzz word USE.

I know he didn't mean anything by it, but it struck a cord in me, a feeling that I had not known since High School. A contempt in which I held the wealthy elite. It was as though I was backed into a corner, I snapped back without thinking.

"Sir, I'm not a person you can use!" Rebutting his last statement, taking it out of context.

Jimmy stood dazed by my outburst, no one had ever spoken to his father like that before. Then finally regaining his composure, he tried to ease the tension that now clothed the room like a blanket. "Calm down! Dad didn't mean…"

"It's ok, son," Mr. Kirtpatrick cut in.

A period of silence fell over the room as Mr. Kirtpatrick and I stared eye to eye, neither one of us wanting to be the first to break the stare.

Jimmy just watched in amazement, unable to intervene, and not sure he wanted to.

"Jimmy," Mr. Kirtpatrick finally broke the silence and stared momentarily. "Would you excuse us for a few moments, I think we need to iron some things out."

Jimmy had seen his father do this before, ever the gentleman in public. But once he had you cornered one on one, he proved quite an adversary. He clearly did not envy my position, and for one brief moment, he thought about taking me out of the room and saving me from the impending lashing that would follow. Yet he didn't, he knew me and trusted his father. Besides, he was more curious than anything else to see who would win the battle of the wills. So Jimmy left the room closing the French doors behind him. Leaving the two bulls to battle it out.

"You don't care for me do you, son?" Mr. Kirtpatrick asked after Jimmy left.

"I care for you just fine, but I'm not your son!" I rebutted with a sarcastic tone.

"Yes, well, I didn't mean anything by what I said

earlier," Mr. Kirtpatrick tried to apologize.

"Maybe not, Sir, and I didn't mean to disrespect you in your home. But I've seen people with money have their way all my life. Looking down on people trying to make it. Throwing them an occasional bone."

"I see," Mr. Kirtpatrick answered, not surprised or insulted by my response. "I would have thought Vietnam would have taken some of that fire out of you, but I guess you always had that fire in your gut."

Pausing for a moment as though to collect his thoughts, while puffing on his cigar, Mr. Kirtpatrick slowly paced the floor.

"You think all this was given to me? I had to work for it, had to fight to keep it. You have a fire in you, a fire I once had, and a fire unfortunately my son doesn't have. My son is by far a smarter businessman than I ever was, but not near as tough. When I'm gone, my enemies will outflank him and destroy both him and the company. I don't want to use you, I need you! I don't have much time," Mr. Kirtpatrick continued to explain. "I'm dying of cancer, I have maybe two months.

I was shocked by this revelation and regretted having attacked him like I had.

"You're Jimmy's friend, he trusts you, and I believe you to be a strong person. I'm asking you to be Jimmy's right hand man, see the things he cannot. As a team, y'all will prove to be invincible."

Does Jimmy know you're dying?" I asked, already saddened for my friend's future loss.

"No, the only one who knows is my wife, and now you," Mr. Kirtpatrick continued to make his case. "My son will need someone like you by his side, I need to know I can count on you."

I paused for a moment then rose from my chair, it was late now, and I graciously shook his hand. "I appreciate your honesty, sir, I'll have an answer for you in the morning."

"Good," Mr. Kirtpatrick replied, sounding confident, or hopeful, I don't know which. Departing to my room, I saw no sign of Jimmy he apparently had gone off to bed. The night was long and I tossed and turned, getting little sleep. Agonizing over what to do. This decision could well effect my life, my future. Why not take it, I reasoned. Other than the fact that it felt like charity. That concern had been put to rest after talking to Mr. Kirtpatrick, I knew I had no other offers and the obvious choice kept coming back around.

CROSSROADS

Chapter 10

I stepped back out of the scene as though plucked from a film in which I once had a part. I looked over to the Angel.

"I remember that night well," I began to reflect, "I ran the gauntlet of every feeling and emotion I knew existed. Until I made my decision."

"Which was?" the Angel asked, as though not knowing the answer.

"I stayed!"

"Yes you did, and as a result, your support was the rock Jimmy needed. Your strong powerful personality insured Jimmy would never be taken advantage of. With you watching out for him, he was able to succeed beyond what anyone had ever envisioned. Y'all proved to be a formidable team.

"But," the Angel paused, "had you chosen differently." The Angel paused as though to give my mind time to catch up. I reflected back on my life often and had always considered the decision I made that day to stay with Jimmy was to be probably the most pivotal point in my whole life. I would always wonder what my life would have been, if I had let stubborn pride stand in the way.

"You would have wandered from job to job,

from city to city, always searching for something you could never find." The Angel cut in just as my thought was finishing. "Finally, you would give up trying to make it in such a competitive world, and drop out."

As he spoke, I could see images of myself flashing rapidly before me, yet my mind absorbed each one as though categorizing the events of a life I never lived. Working in various jobs, the kaleidoscope of images continued, so did the Angel's explanation.

"Finally," he continued, "you would live on the streets finding your meals in garbage bins. And your bed, a cardboard box. For many years, you would endure this life, each day turning you more and more bitter to the society that you felt let you down. When you finally would reach rock bottom and your pride no longer could sustain you, you would seek help, but no help could be found, your family was all gone. Your best friend, Jimmy, as you would find out much, later was also gone. His once thriving business failed and he ended up losing all he had. Once his money was gone, so was his wife. He ended up taking his own life.

"You, however, would live much longer to the age of fifty-two when pneumonia finally took a fatal grasp on you. You would die; bitter, broken, and alone."

As I pondered my possible fate. I shook, as a chill

came over me. One decision had made such a difference, I thought, reflecting on a life that never was.

"Let us move forward now," the Angel said, dragging me forward through time, when we eventually came to a stop, it was many years later.

CROSSROADS

Chapter 11

I saw myself now, much older, more mature, I held a campaign poster in my hand. I remembered the time. My first race for political office. The race that catapulted me to heights I had never dreamed.

As Jimmy's father had predicted, Jimmy and I proved to be a tremendous team. Side by side through the years, we struggled and fought many battles together, and for the most part came out of top. We had transformed a small family-owned operation into a Fortune 500 company in less than twenty years. I had become wealthier than I had ever dreamed. Money was no longer an issue in my life. I would fall in love with Jimmy's sister Emily and have two children. I was truly fulfilled for a while.

With the business on an even keel and Jimmy and I having picked up many of each other's personality traits, I was no longer a vital part of the business, at least that's the way I felt. I had to seek new challenges and not having the burden of having to make a living, I decided to dedicate myself to public service.

The road proved far easier than I would have imagined. I had an inherent gift for gab and charisma and charm, which could soften even the most vocal opponents. Yet beyond all the charm and smooth talking, I still retained the values of a common man. Though I could hardly be able to be considered common with the wealth I had been able to amass, I would never forget where I came from. When I traveled the countryside, I could relate to each and every one of the people I met, rich and poor it didn't matter, for at one point in my life I stood where they stood. I have seen the world through their eyes. I think in part this is what

made me such a successful politician. The other part being, I had the financial backing needed to run a campaign, Jimmy saw to that. Each race I entered, he pulled out all stops, called in favors when necessary, anything that was required he did. With those two things working for me, I proved to be very successful.

"And successful you were," the Angel spoke out choosing not to downplay the significance of those days, as I had.

"One house races and two senate races, all won by landslides. Then, finally, the decision to run for president. Do you remember that day?" the Angel asked as the image of myself contemplating that decision so many years earlier came into view.

"You would pay a heavy price for the responsibility you sought, and many, many times, you questioned yourself as to whether or not you made the right choice."

the Angel's voice was conciliatory, being able to see all that I had seen and knowing all that I had known.

"So let's look now on what might have been." The Angel began setting the stage for a time never seen, and a life never lived. Poised on a precipice of a crossroad, down an unused path into events that never happened ... but could have.

The serenity, which I had grown accustomed to after each scene, quickly fell away. It was as though the bottom literally fell out. Falling into a rapidly swirling vortex of dark storm clouds, I twirled topsy-turvy. Lightning flashed, followed by ear-piecing thunder, accompanied by a flash of an image. An image of a life never seen. Then, as suddenly as it had began, the vortex disappeared and I found myself in what appeared to be a fog bank, and there was silence once more. It was as though walking through a door. One side peaceful, calm, and silent, but as soon as you crossed the threshold, you stepped into the violent storm of chaos.

As I walked through the fog, it began to thin, until it completely evaporated, revealing a scene that I had no memory of, though I was in the scene. I was slowly being pulled toward myself by an unseen force, which I only halfheartedly resisted. I knew from the previous series of events that what was to be seen was inevitable. Besides, I thought, this is what I had longed for all my life! To go down a path I had often wondered about. A crossroad in my life that had haunted me, even to this point.

Chapter 12

Campaigning came into view as I shook hand after hand. "I remember," I replied to the Angel's question. It proved to be a hard-fought battle and I would pay a heavy price with my family. The campaign for President proved to be a miserable experience, hundreds of times greater than that of senator. Hopping from town to town, never twice in the same bed. My commitment drove a wedge between my family, as my wife and I slowly drifted apart, until we were no more than strangers. My children did not fare much better. Not having the support and guidance of their father, our kids sought to rebel. Whereas we were able to regain control of our daughter, our son continued to spiral into the dark regions of drugs until finally it cost him his young life. Oh, how I regretted those days, the way I felt when I saw his body in the casket then finally lowered into his grave. My heart was ripped out, incapable of feeling any longer. My wife and I split up some time later, unable to bridge the gorge that had placed itself between us. It was with this backdrop I entered the White House. The first President in history ever to hold the office unmarried.

I watched and remembered as I wiped the tears from my eye. I had run that scenario through my mind many times and wondered what might have been if only I had not become President, I remembered praying to see the path not chosen. To see if my son would have lived. "Oh Angel, let me see," I pleaded. "Please let me see what might have been. I beg you."

"You shall see," he said as again the kaleidoscope of images faced before me, each appearing in chronological order. Events that would have transpired if I had not run for President. I saw my children graduate from college and embarking on careers of their own, but hindered by a recession that dwarfed the great depression. My kids and family were intact, and the wealth we had amassed over the years let us ride this storm out. But as I looked on, I saw a country in shambles drowning in red ink. Entire agencies shut down. Unemployment soared, as bread-lines formed for the first time since the Great Depression. Urban decay festered, and crime was rapid as the country teetered on anarchy. Finally, with all social fabric destroyed, the 'have-nots' the people hungry and struggling to survive turned toward the people of means.

Our home was destroyed along with our lives. Oh, how tragic a fate, as to be the last to die watching each one of your family die before you.

I looked on in shock, I had always envisioned a far different scenario when I had played it through my mind's eye. How could this have happened just because I didn't become President? "Don't you see," the Angel asked, "the country would face turbulent times ahead. Without your vision and determinations to pull us through, we all would perish."

"How can one man do so much?"

"You were not alone," the Angel said. "Remember the path you chose," he said, pointing to the image that came into view.

CROSSROADS

Chapter 13

It seemed no sooner had I been sworn into office than the trouble began. The economy began to slow, with interest rates soaring. Creating the interest payment on the debt far greater than anyone could have even imagined. No confidence in the dollar sent it plummeting to record lows. Banks began to fail on a scale not seen since the eighties.

I knew I had to act quickly and through Executive Order, I froze all assets from all countries. This would buy only a little time, for I knew the lawyers would be knocking down doors fighting to see who could get to the Supreme Court first.

Next, I held an emergency meeting to address congress, which was carried on every TV and radio station across the country.

"My fellow Americans," I started out, "we stand on the verge of our entire way of life disappearing. An implosion of our economy, our legal system, banking, and even our government is eminent if we do not take drastic steps to correct this. This is not a time for partisanship. History has proven that when this country is faced with great diversity, we have always banded together for the common good, a common cause.

"I face you gentlemen to say to you this will be the days to which you metal will be tested. Your character called upon. For without you, our nation, our republic will die. There will be no foreign powers rolling tanks down Pennsylvania Avenue. Only a line of limousines escorting the new owners to view their property. The cost will be high, the sacrifice great. But the only alternative is not an option. I shall stand beside any man here and lay my life down for this country. For that is what must happen if we should fail.

"Within a week, I will have a plan that will take steps to resolve this crisis. As we speak, a panel of leading economists are searching for a solution. With God's help, we shall overcome this challenge, like we have meet so many others for so many years. We have defended the word while they concentrated on building their economy. Today, we embark on a policy of defending ourselves. After, and only after, our security is ensured both militarily and economically, will we begin to rejoin the world as a defender."

Executive Order 310 ensured the recall of all foreign military personnel. During this period, the domestic situation had worsened and crime was on the rise. I knew whatever I did, I would be sued by lawyers. I had but one option. I had to do what no other president in the history of the union had to do, I did what many thought was unthinkable: I suspended the constitution and declared martial law. Order would be restored. Returning military personnel were not discharged, the economy was too overburden as it was. They were retrained as police support. The effects overseas of our troops withdrawing sent many nations rushing into the arms build up, creating a tremendous export of military hardware overseas, nothing of which was seen since World War Two, which in time gave the economy a much-boosted shot in the arm. Next, we faced the twenty trillion-dollar debt that faced our nation.

The options were few, Japan backed ninety percent of our debt, and to wipe the slate clean, a bargain would have to be struck with Japan.

To the sorrows of many and the dissent of all, a deal was struck with Japan. We would provide for Japan's security for twenty years at the cost of the United States.

Also, the Hawaiian Islands would be sold completely to Japan and, with the exception of the Memorial at Pearl Harbor, would be under Japanese rule. This was the hardest pill many Americans had to swallow. It was the first time in our history we actually had to sell a piece of property to a foreign power. Yet it was necessary.

With our debt cleared and the tremendous export of arms, our economy soared to record heights and the dollar was once again strong.

The constitution was restored, and military personal were discharged to a growing economy.

The economy had turned around, but crime was still

on the rise so Legislature was passed through Congress and a practical death penalty was implemented. Death row throughout the country was purged, to screaming objections of the Liberal lawyers, who used the appeal system only to line their pockets.

The cheers of millions of law-abiding people who finally saw the justice system working muffled their objections. Criminals, though poorly educated for the most part, are by no means dumb. When they saw a system of justice that no longer coddled the criminal, crime took a drastic decline.

During this time, there were moves for my impeachment, but the initiators of such a move soon realized the support I had amassed for these sweeping polices. And they themselves had been the ones in retreat, trying to escape being tarred and feathered by a livid constituency.

Prison systems were next privatized, with the only demands placed on prisons was that they be fed, clothed, and forced to perform menial labor for the states. The cost of running prisons in this country plummeted and the prison system suddenly lost its appeal. No TV, no hot tubs. Just work, sleep and do your time.

The United States was once again strong, we had

regained control of our borders by the use of the military deployed all along Mexico.

Mexico immediately objected, but once they saw we meant business, they backed down.

We were now prepared to join the world once more. We were strong, vibrant and powerful. The combined efforts of all economic markets formulated a plan to join the world as one. The United Nations would be restructured and given greater control of international, when aggressive nations got out of hand. Each country would remain in control of their domestic affairs. The biggest change would be a world currency. This would straighten the offset between currency yen and dollar.

Currency would display Nobel Prize winners thereby giving the currency neutral appeal.

All this was accomplished and after twenty years, it has performed magnificently. I understood then what the Angel meant, how one person could make a difference.

Once again, the Angel pulled me back from the scene. Over what had seemed such a short time, I had visited all the major crossroads of my life. Through luck or destiny, I resolved within myself that I had chosen the crossroads correctly. In the end, all we truly leave behind our deeds, good or bad.

CROSSROADS

As I looked upon the Angel, I realized the time was at hand, all that was for me to do on this Earth had been done. As I reached my outstretched hand toward the Angel, for the first time, I felt a sudden warmth as the glow of the Angel's face started to lessen, revealing facial features. Soon, his image was clear, my guide in the crossroads of my life had been none other than my own beloved son, who I had feared I would never see again. I embraced him as a sudden surge of energy filled my body.

"Let's go home, Father," he said as he led me upward.

The flower-clad room now lay empty as the line on the heart monitor had straightened now, and a sheet was pulled over Hill's spiritless corpse. Life had departed?

www.ingramcontent.com/pod-product-compliance
Lightning Source LLC
Chambersburg PA
CBHW020620250626
47154CB00004B/1597